ALL THE WAY

by ANDY BEHRENS

DUTTON BOOKS • New York

DUTTON BOOKS
A member of Penguin Group (USA) Inc.

Published by the Penguin Group
Penguin Group (USA) Inc., 375 Hudson Street, New York, New York 10014, U.S.A.
Penguin Group (Canada), 90 Eglinton Avenue East, Suite 700, Toronto, Ontario, Canada M4P 2Y3
(a division of Pearson Penguin Canada Inc.)
Penguin Books Ltd, 80 Strand, London WC2R 0RL, England
Penguin Ireland, 25 St Stephen's Green, Dublin 2, Ireland (a division of Penguin Books Ltd)
Penguin Group (Australia), 250 Camberwell Road, Camberwell, Victoria 3124, Australia
(a division of Pearson Australia Group Pty Ltd)
Penguin Books India Pvt Ltd, 11 Community Centre, Panchsheel Park, New Delhi - 110 017, India
Penguin Group (NZ), Cnr Airborne and Rosedale Roads, Albany, Auckland 1310, New Zealand
(a division of Pearson New Zealand Ltd)
Penguin Books (South Africa) (Pty) Ltd, 24 Sturdee Avenue, Rosebank, Johannesburg 2196, South Africa
Penguin Books Ltd, Registered Offices: 80 Strand, London WC2R 0RL, England

CIP data is available.

Published in the United States by Dutton Books, a member of Penguin Group (USA) Inc.
375 Hudson Street, New York, New York 10014
www.penguin.com/youngreaders

Produced by Alloy Entertainment
ALLOYENTERTAINMENT   151 West 26th Street
New York, New York 10001

Designed by Joel Tippie

Printed in USA
First Edition

ISBN 0-525-47761-6
1 3 5 7 9 10 8 6 4 2

The writer would like to extend his sincere thanks to all those who have helped either with this project specifically, or with his writing career in general. This list includes, but is not limited to, James Norton, Lynn Weingarten, Eric Neel, Chris Sprow, Jada Carson, Eric Wittmershaus, the proprietors of the Caribou Coffee at 2453 N. Clark Street, the editorial staff at the Chicago Reader, the good people at Dutton Books, Tim Courtney, Chris Harris, the Garg family, Mom and Dad, and—of course—the delightful Jennifer Boss and Ella Behrens.

This day is gonna suck, thought Ian Lafferty.

He pulled his car into its usual spot, underneath a willow tree near one of the least-trafficked entrances to Fox Valley Mall. It was just after 6:30 A.M. on a Thursday in late August. Ian was sleepy, unshowered, and arriving at work just late enough to irritate his manager.

He stepped out of his preposterously large car—an aged yellow Oldsmobile that Ian had a deep affection for and that his friends had dubbed "the Creature"—into the thick air of a steamy morning. He sighed, then trudged across the parking lot, stumbling through a planting bed full of ferns, and unlocked an employees-only doorway. Inside, he walked slowly toward the food court beneath a canopy of decorative mall foliage. He pulled his Dunkin' Donuts cap low over his eyes. He watched his shadow drift across the dark storefronts of Hot Topic, Abercrombie, Origins—places, it occurred to him, where the employees weren't forced to arrive at ungodly times just to serve

\

éclairs to mall-walkers. Not that Ian disliked mall-walkers. No, they were actually among his favorite customers. But he strongly disliked 6:30 A.M.

This whole summer has sucked, he thought.

The galactic suckiness of his summer was made all the more apparent by the fact that his closest friends, Felicia Alpine and Lance Nesbitt, had been having a spectacular time far away from Naperville, Illinois. Felicia was traveling along the Mediterranean with her family, and Lance was working for his uncle rehabbing homes (in a toil-at-your-own-slow-pace capacity, Ian suspected) in some idyllic little Michigan resort town. Their absence left Ian with a social life that had become weapons-grade boring. Ian's father had insisted that his seventeen-year-old son get a job instead of inhabiting the Lafferty basement all summer. That mandate had led him to Dunkin' Donuts.

Ian's dad hadn't forced him to specifically work at Fox Valley, of course. No, that had been Ian's choice. For some reason, he'd thought it would help him—or force him—to meet new people. Exotic mall girls, maybe. And Ian could speak to them using the pretext of food service: "Can I help you, miss? Wow, that's a cool toe ring. Is it from Claire's? Would you like a scone?" Or something like that. Unfortunately, exotic mall girls did not seem to patronize Dunkin' Donuts. The lone exception to this rule was a small, dark-haired girl named Laila who operated the mall's merry-go-round. (Maybe *operate* was too strong a verb for what Laila did. She flipped a switch on and off and rang a bell.) Laila had been a faithful consumer since early June, ordering two raspberry-filled doughnuts and a caramel swirl latte on her break every afternoon. Predisposed as he was to falling for a mall girl, Ian soon developed a crush on her. Their relationship went exactly like every other crush in Ian's life had gone: he quickly befriended Laila, and she began talking to him about how much she liked some other dude. In Laila's case, the other dude was an insensitive, obnoxious coworker named Flynn. By early July, she had expanded her daily order to include two powdered-sugar doughnuts and an iced espresso. These were for Flynn. At some point, they started dating. By early August, Laila had replaced her daily doughnuts and latte with a simple banana and a Diet Pepsi. Flynn, it seemed, had called her "pudgy," and he had gotten just a little too flirty with some scrawny waif who worked at Lady Foot Locker. Laila became utterly weight-obsessed. Ian repeatedly told her she looked great, to which she said things like, "No, Flynn's right. I'm a house. A big, fat house, with a deck and a three-car garage." How totally depressing, Ian thought, to give up doughnuts. For anyone. Laila looked way prettier, Ian had thought, with a wide smile and a raspberry doughnut than with an anxious frown and a diet cola. A few pounds either way didn't change a thing. But Flynn apparently disagreed, and he occupied the boyfriend chair.

Ian glanced at his watch.

Oh, crap.

Suddenly aware that he was much later for work than he'd meant to be, he descended the stairs that led to the food court with a series of noisy, graceless leaps. He tucked a few strands of longish brown hair beneath his hat. He rushed past the unlit signs of Arby's, McDonald's, Taco Bell, and Panda Express, then heard a shrill voice echoing across the tiled floor.

"Glad you could make it in today, buddy!" said Ron Fleschman, longtime doughnut shop manager. "Seven minutes late. Ian Lafferty's employee-of-the-month chances take yet another hit."

"Sorry, Ron," he offered. "Had a late night."

That wasn't a lie, exactly. But it suggested just the sort of nocturnal deviance that Ian's life sadly lacked. In fact, he had stayed awake until nearly 2 A.M. grazing on Fritos, slaying mythical creatures on his Xbox, and listening to Radiohead. So yeah, late night. Woo.

Ron licked powdered sugar from his plump fingers, then began shuffling crullers with plastic tongs.

"Start a pot of decaf, Ian."

He nodded, peeled a coffee filter from its stack, and began to spoon dark granules into the industrial Bunn-o-Matic. His phone began to ring. (It was more than a phone, actually. It was a Toady 2.0, the newest too-expensive wafer-thin must-have wireless contraption. Ian had recently blown a portion of his Donut savings on the device. With the Toady, he could phone, IM, text, and e-mail. He suspected that he could also use it to cook meat, eviscerate aliens, and control the weather. It really had a lot of tiny buttons.) He extracted the Toady from his pocket.

Who the hell calls this early?

Ron gave him a quizzical look that morphed into a stern glare. Again, Ian did not particularly care.

He looked at the caller ID. The number had a 231 area code, which meant it was almost certainly Lance. Ian answered the call as Ron continued to stare.

"Hello, Lance."

He heard only indistinct chatter, laughing, and music.

"Hello?" he repeated.

"Duuuuuuude!" said a familiar and slightly sloshed voice. "What's happening? Whadja do last night, buddy?"

"Nothing. Stayed in." He paused, watching Ron fold his arms across his massive belly in an attempt to appear menacing. "I've got doughnuts and coffee to sell, Lance. What's up? I'm guessing you had a good night."

"Dude, I'm *still* having a good night," he said. "Haven't gone to sleep yet!" More background laughing. It was clearly a girl's voice. "This place rocks. Best summer job ever. So—"

"You make me sick, Lance."

"—the reason I'm calling is that—"

"Seriously. Physically sick."

"—I gotta know that we're still—"

"Like with vomit."

"—on for this weekend!"

Dead silence. Ian fumbled with the bag of coffee, spilling it across the countertop and eliciting an exasperated sigh from his manager. Ron muttered to himself, belched, plucked a powdered-sugar doughnut from its display rack, and took a bite.

"This weekend," said Ian, distracted. "This weekend . . ."

"Lance-a-Palooza, dude! It's a summer tradition. You, me, Felicia. My cousin is totally expecting us. There's an all-ages show at the Metro on Saturday. The Air and Water Show is going on at North Avenue Beach. It'll be sweet."

Ian remained silent, scooping up coffee with his hands and returning it to the bag. He hadn't forgotten Lance-a-Palooza, though he wasn't prepared to commit. Not while there was still a possibility, however unlikely, that his weekend might offer something riskier and far more titillating—something he wasn't yet prepared to discuss with Lance. Or anyone else. But Lance-a-Palooza was, as Lance had said, a summer tradition. For three consecutive years, on the weekend before classes resumed at Naperville Polytechnic High School, Ian, Felicia, and Lance had left their suburb to spend a lost weekend in Chicago with Lance's feckless cousin Doug. Naturally, Lance had named the event after himself.

He continued to prod Ian.

"C'mon. Like Ian Lafferty could possibly miss the only remotely social thing he does between June and September. You're still in, right? I'm driving home tonight. I figured we'd cruise into the city to-morrow." Then, away from the receiver, Lance said, "Not that I couldn't be convinced to stay awhile . . ."

A muffled wet squelching sound was followed by more female laughter. Then Lance returned to the phone.

"So, Ian, you can drive us in the Creature, right? When does Felicia get back, dude? Have you heard from her?"

"Um, no . . ." Ian said. "I haven't talked to Felicia since—wait, why do I have to drive? Why can't you dri–?"

Ron inched toward Ian, scowling. "We'll have customers in fifteen minutes, Ian! The mall-walkers! Many of them like to enjoy a flavor-ful decaffeinated beverage while they exercise." He stifled another belch with his meaty fist.

Ian continued, peeved at Lance. "Why can't you drive us?"

"We can't risk the Mazda's health in city traffic. You drive, like, a fifty-dollar car."

"In its prime, it was a luxury automobile. And anyway, I bought it for three *hundred* and fifty dol—"

"So you're coming. Great. Excellent news. I can't wait. Listen, dude . . ." More giggly girl sounds. "I really need to go."

Ian heard a rustling sound over the line, followed by a quick laugh, then a tipsy female voice.

"Helloooo?" it said.

"Um . . . hello. Who's this?" Ian asked.

"Lance's last fling of the summer, I think. Although he's still in town for a few more hours, so who really knows . . . ?" The voice trailed off into what sounded like a smooch, presumably with Lance.

Several awkward seconds passed. Ian almost hung up. Except that he was mesmerized, not having actually kissed any girl, ever. None that he remembered kissing, at any rate. There *had* been the disastrous Felicia/Pabst/plastic deer episode of sophomore year, but he didn't consider that a romantic interlude so much as a personal tragedy. Near the end of the first unabashedly drunken night of their lives, Ian and Felicia had apparently kissed. Or so he'd been told by semi-reliable witnesses. Ian didn't have any specific memory of the incident, and he'd never discussed it with Felicia herself. The evening had ended with Ian professing his undying love to a plastic lawn deer, vomiting on said deer, and then falling asleep at its plastic hooves. All in all, a very bad night.

Lance and the sloshed girl continued their somewhat more traditional smooch for several seconds before she returned to the phone.

"Hey, are you anything like Lancey?" she asked. "Do you, like, have a girlfriend?"

"No. Nothing like him. And no girlfriend."

Ian heard Lance's voice in the background: "Ian's a *nice* boy." As if *nice* were a dirty word. This was one of Lance's favorite conversational forays: teasing Ian for being too responsible, too friendly, too emotive, too . . . well, just too *sweet* to attract girls. Ian usually rolled his eyes at such advice, but, silently, he'd taken it to heart. After all, he did want to be liked by girls. Or at least noticed.

Ron coughed purposefully, eyeing Ian, and tapped a finger on his wristwatch. The girl continued talking.

"You know, Ian," said the girl on the phone, "there's something to be said for guys who are maybe not always so considerate. Like your jerky friend here." Ian merely listened. "I mean, does he ever call me? No. Does he take me out? Of course not. But does he expect me to steal my parents' booze and meet him in an empty vacation house where we can do, um . . ."

More smooching sounds.

". . . stuff? Yes." She sighed. "And do I do it?"

Still more smooching sounds.

"Yes."

"Why?" Ian asked, frustrated. "He's not *that* adorable."

Lance took the phone.

"I'm sure that being a totally nice guy like yourself has its advantages, Ian. And you should tell me about 'em sometime. But try being Mister Not-so-nice Guy once in a while. Just with the occasional hot chick. See where it takes you."

Egotistical jerk. Inconsiderate prick.

More smooching noises.

Lucky bastard.

Lance Nesbitt's ability to attract girls was, Ian thought, truly un-canny. He was good looking enough—chronically tan, naturally ath-letic, the owner of a charming smile—but his physical appearance didn't seem to be the essence of his appeal. It just didn't get in the way. Lance was confident, clever, and cheerful—never reserved. He was a high-volume flirter who brushed off rejection easily, and, it seemed to Ian, had an innate sense for when to compliment a girl and when to tease her. He had a knack for quickly becoming the social hub of any room. There was a certain sort of female—and they tended to be incredibly beautiful—whom Lance could woo, conquer, and dis-miss with startling efficiency. Not that Ian had ever *wanted* to treat girls like that—the conquering and dismissing parts always seemed like they would have left him feeling guilty and sad. But being able to woo when the situation called for wooing was something Ian had al-ways wished he was capable of.

"I don't know how you can stand to be such an a-hole, Lance. And I don't know *why* a certain subset of girls seems to prefer it."

"No? So you're gonna stay honest and chivalrous your whole life?"

Ian said nothing. He had, in fact, been conducting a little experi-ment that required him to be a bit less honest and chivalrous. But he wasn't ready to discuss his results with Lance just yet.

"C'mon, Ian. How's the nice-guy thing been working out for you? With girls, I mean. Have you *polited* your way into any dates?"

Again, Ian said nothing.

Ron had become apoplectic, a quivering, middle-aged blob of hostility. He extended his watch to within inches of Ian's face.

"Listen, Lance," said Ian, eyeing his manager, "the doughnuts are calling."

"Later, dude. I'll see you tomorrow."

"Yeah, about tha—"

Click.

Ron quickly lit into him.

"I swear, Lafferty, you're lucky your father is my dentist! I'd have fired you by now. Twice! You're always on the phone. Or typing away on your little gadgets."

Ron sighed, then wiped his hands on the front of his shirt, leaving streaks of powdered sugar across his chest. "Finish cleaning off these countertops. And please, no more spills. I need to check on a few things."

He stalked off into the back room, where he often became engrossed in games of computer solitaire while pretending to review work-related spreadsheets.

Ian began spritzing the counter with cleaning solution. Within seconds, his Toady rang again. He answered it quickly, without checking to see who was calling—he assumed it was either Lance or Lance's newest "friend."

"Jeez! Enough! I get it. Lance Nesbitt is a stud, I'm a geek. I'm already in such deep shit for talking to you. So what the—"

"Um, hi, Ian." The connection was poor, but the voice on the line was unmistakably Felicia's.

"Did you miss me?" she asked.

"Oh, God. Oh. Sorry, Felicia. Are you finally home?" Ian was whispering, peering into the back room to confirm that Ron was indeed testing his limited wits against the doughnut shop's ancient PC and thus oblivious to the world.

"No, I'm in the airport in Paris. Hope I'm not calling too early. It's afternoon here, and our flight's in, like, twenty minutes. And I'm bored as hell. I called my aunt. She's watching my dog. I talked to the dog for a while. It was nice. And now I'm calling you. Bored, bored, bored . . ."

"Yeah, same here. But I don't have a dog to call. I'm at work. The mall's about to open. The walkers are about to line up for coffee."

"Oooh, are they cuties? Do they wear Rockports? And pants with elastic waistbands?"

"Something like that. They're pretty cute." He paused. "And yeah, I missed you." He paused again. "I mean, the collective you. You and Lance. You know . . . things have been a little dull."

"I missed you, too."

"So you're back tonight?" Ian asked.

"Yup, and soooo ready to go downtown tomorrow. I have *got* to get away from my family."

Ian wilted. Whereas the promise of three straight Lance-filled days did not necessarily thrill him, he wanted very much to see Felicia. Almost desperately. But there were other plans already in motion.

An office chair rolled and creaked in the back room. Ron was moving.

"Crap. Not trying to be a jerk, Felicia, but my boss can't see me on the phone again. Gotta run. Call me when you get in. Whenever. I'll be up."

"Actually, Ian, can I come over when I get ba–?"

Click.

Yup, that day pretty much sucked, thought Ian.

In the late-afternoon heat, he loped slowly toward his car, which sat, covered in bird poop, in the shade of the willow tree. His workday was over.

As usual, his interaction with the early-morning walkers had indeed been the highlight of his day. The Silver Sole Sisters—a particularly loveable trio of mall-walking eightysomethings who dressed in matching rayon sweat suits—had squeezed his face and complimented his manners. Ian quite liked them. He greeted them warmly, poured their decafs, and laughed at their jokes. They offered to introduce him to their various granddaughters: "Oh, Ian, you really should meet my Diane. She's so pretty but always bringing home such dreadful boys."

"That would be lovely, Mrs. Hagwood," he said.

When the Sole Sisters left Dunkin' Donuts, Ian's day went to crap. He spent the rest of his morning shoveling cholesterol and caffeine across the counter to gruff mall employees and busy shoppers. Then, around noon, he slipped into a giant foam doughnut suit and distributed scratch-and-win coupons throughout the mall. This was his least-favorite workplace activity. Ian had done it not at the request of his manager but as a favor to his coworker, Becca, who usually wore the suit—Ron preferred having a pretty blonde represent the franchise—but hadn't wanted to do it on this particular Thursday. She had a date with a boy from the Gap after work and didn't want to smell, as she described it, "poopacious." The doughnut smelled like the worst possible combination of Lysol, excessive sweat, and sugar. Very poopacious. But Ian had agreed to wear it. He agreed to nearly everything Becca, or anyone else, asked of him.

"You're *such* a great friend," she'd said. "You're so sweet."

He heard Lance's voice in his head: "How's the nice-guy thing been working out for you? With girls, I mean."

Not well. Not well at all.

So, by the end of his day, Ian was completely spent. His eyes were half shut as he hit the parking lot. It was only when he reached the Creature, unlocked the door, and began to sit down that he realized he'd never actually changed out of the giant doughnut.

"Oh, shit," he said, just loud enough to draw a surprised look from a woman passing by with a stroller.

The stroller's occupant excitedly declared, "Mom, that doughnut said the *s* word! He really did, Mom! Is it okay for big doughnuts to say the *s* word, Mom?"

"No, honey, it's not. It's not okay for you, grown-ups, or big doughnuts to say it."

Ian slammed his car door, then scrunched up the foam so that he could sit properly. He'd intended to drop the suit off at DD before leaving but, in his rush to be anywhere but the food court, he had forgotten.

He started the car, then flipped on the air conditioner. He picked up a Baby Ruth that he'd left on the passenger seat. It felt partially melted, but he was starving. He fumbled for a CD underneath the seat, selecting a mix that Felicia had given him at Christmas, then tore open the candy bar wrapper. He raised the candy bar to his mouth, then watched it sag, break, and fall toward his lap and onto the doughnut, where it left a trail of melted chocolate across the foam. The half-Ruth plopped onto the driver's side floor mat.

"Oops," Ian said, eating the other half.

He put the car in reverse, then, recalling that there was still one thing that might allow him to salvage some pleasure from the wreckage of his day, he threw the Creature back into park. He pulled his Toady from his pocket to check his e-mail—not the first time that day he'd done so. There were two messages. The first was from Lance.

To: ilafferty@toady.com, feliciousalp@yahoo.com
CC: dougthebarbarian@hotmail.com
From: lanceinmypants@msn.com
Subject: Lance-a-Palooza!!!

It. Is. On.

Oh yes, it is on. We ride at dawn on Friday. (OK,
maybe dawn is too early. Let's say 10-ish?) We'll
make it to Doug's by noon. Hopefully it won't
take Ian too long to park his boat. I've
thoughtfully taken care of all your beer and fake
ID needs. Pack light.

Felicia, hope you had a great summer. Ian, I
know you had a lame summer. So prepare
yourself. Because . . .

It. Is. On.

What Lance didn't realize, and could have never possibly guessed, was that, despite the general lameness of his summer, Ian *had* managed to meet a girl. In fact, he'd met her just the previous week. Her name was Danielle. And Danielle was going to be, with any luck at all, the reason that Ian couldn't attend Lance-a-Palooza. Even though he felt sort of bad about it, Ian had attracted her using Lance's methods. That is, he'd been a callous, manipulative jerk when necessary, only exhibiting sweetness when Danielle expected it least or needed it most.

The next e-mail on Ian's Toady was from her:

To: ilafferty@toady.com
From: dmorrison@scsu.edu
Subject: Re: Re: road trip?

Oh, you HAVE to come! Pleeease?! Pretty please?
I'm leaving Monday night. And yes, I'll make the
trip worth it. You won't be disappointed.
Promise. ;)

D

Ian felt his stomach tighten and he bit his lip. Was it possible it was really this easy? After all the years of rejection, rejection, and rejection . . .

He backed up the car, steered onto the inner drive of the mall, and headed for home.

He had met Danielle Morrison online, at DunkinDisorderly.com, a Web site for aggrieved DD employees. Her screen name was BoredyVonBoredenstein. They'd encountered each other in a chat session and had soon begun texting and IMing. Ian found that communicating this way suited him well. When he spoke to people in person—especially to girls—he felt scared, nervous, and dorky. But when he wrote—especially to Danielle—he felt free, uninhibited, and sure of himself. Or rather, "himself." It was unusually easy writing to her, because he wasn't being himself, at all. He referred to her as "Miss Tasty." (He had lifted the name from a disturbingly funny cable documentary called *The Pimp-tastic Voyage* that he and Danielle had been watching the night they first chatted. In the documentary, Miss Tasty was a hunchbacked meth-addicted transvestite prostitute who lived somewhere in the South. Ian immediately began teasing Danielle that she probably looked something like him/her, and so he shouldn't waste his time flirting with her. Danielle responded by sending Ian several pictures—a revealing series of beach pictures, actually—that proved she was quite the opposite of a malformed she-male ho. She was, in fact, gorgeous.). Ian had become quickly infatuated with Danielle. Or at least infatuated with their communication.

He'd broken out every move he could remember from the Lance Nesbitt picking-up-chicks handbook. When Ian wasn't strategically ignoring Danielle, he was ridiculing her grammar, her troubles, her school (South Carolina Southern University in Charleston), her politics (right-leaning), her car (a Cabriolet)—he ridiculed *her*, basically. He squelched his natural aversion to treating someone so carelessly by telling himself over and over that no one was forcing her to write to him. She could stop at any time, right? But, amazingly, she didn't stop. And for some reason that Ian couldn't understand, she seemed always to come back for more. At some point Ian had claimed to be a student at Northwestern—a soon-to-be sophomore, just like her. He'd sent her a heavily Photoshopped digital picture of himself. It was still Ian Lafferty, but a tricked-out version: stylized, slick, tan, and capable of growing facial hair. It had all been intended as a harmless deception, really. Just an online flirtation.

Then she invited him to visit.

Initially, he ignored her. Then she begged him. She wrote to say that she was leaving soon to spend a semester in Spain and she just *had* to meet him. He found the thought of meeting her tempting, very tempting. But Ian also felt a creeping sort of guilt about misrepresenting himself. He'd never actually expected to know Danielle offline, live and in person. He deflected her invitations, dismissed her pleas. He claimed she couldn't possibly be serious. Danielle insisted that she was. She told him in an IM that it was time they **m00ved 2 the next level**. Ian found this both exhilarating and terrifying. He didn't know anything about the next level. He didn't commit. He called her a tease. She wrote, **Moi? Mizz Tasty? A tease? I'll show U teasing. . . .**

She sent him more beach pictures. Utterly jaw-dropping, smokin' hot beach pictures, thought Ian. But remaining in Lance mode, he told her that he wasn't going to travel all the way from Illinois to South Carolina "just to take you to dinner. I can take local girls to dinner." That comment had led to the e-mail he'd just received, assuring him that he wouldn't be disappointed.

And with that, he was determined to drive to Charleston. Urgently. Like, the following day. He would e-mail Danielle to confirm the details, but not just yet—he was often deliberately slow in responding to her. It was no easy thing for a permanently girlfriendless teenage virgin whose own lack of experience caused him incredible amounts of embarrassment and shame—and in fact at times made him feel like a *freak*—to appear coolly ambivalent when an attractive girl promised sex. But for the online alter ego he had cultivated, it came quite naturally.

Ian pulled into his cul-de-sac, past rows of young trees, and into his family's driveway. He entered the house through the garage, discarded the fallen half of the candy bar, grabbed a Yoo-hoo from the fridge, and walked into the living room, where his father sat with his feet on an ottoman and his head concealed by the sports section of the *Chicago Tribune*.

"Hi, Dad. Where's Mom?"

"Health club. Or Costco. Or maybe it was the health club first, then Costco."

"Short day today?"

"My last cleaning canceled on me."

His father lowered the paper. Larry Lafferty, like Ian, was an angular man with dark, unruly hair. He gave Ian his most serious look, and Ian was certain he knew what was coming.

"I saw the x-rays, Ian." Larry Lafferty shook his head. "Your appointment yesterday? Two cavities? Jee-*zuhs*." He raised the paper again. "If you don't start flossing and the condition of your gums doesn't improve, you can find yourself a new dentist, Ian. That's all I can say."

"Sorry, Dad. I will." Ian took a long sip from the Yoo-hoo. "I'll floss, that is."

After a heavy silence, Ian's father said, "Your mother and I leave for the conference early tomorrow morning. Are you working?"

"Nope, I'm off. I'll be in the city with Lance and Felicia, remember?"

He was tickled that his parents would be at the North American Dental Association conference in Las Vegas. While Ian was driving toward his first sexual experience, they'd be drinking, gambling, learning whatever they didn't already know about molars, and would be blissfully unconcerned about their sneaky son's whereabouts.

"Oh yeah. Lance-a-rama or whatever. Right. You really should've had the oil changed on the Creature. It's been a while." He paused. "Shouldn't you be working, by the way?"

Ian peered down the full length of his chocolate-smeared doughnut costume, and gave his father a What-the-hell-do-you-*want*-from-me? sort of look. His father shrugged.

"Okay, so maybe you could use a little break before school starts. Your mother prepared a few meals for you for the weekend." He thought for a moment. "Actually, she prepared six different meals, I think. All your lunches and dinners. They're in the fridge in numbered cartons. You can take them with you this weekend."

Ian shook his head. "Wake me before you guys leave, all right?"

His dad said, "Mmmmm," and delved further into the paper.

Ian thought that just maybe, if he could hit the road early, before Lance could pester him again, he could avoid having to (a) tell his friends about Danielle or (b) lie to their faces. He detested the idea of misleading his friends.

Ian's Toady jangled. As he marched off toward his room, he looked at the caller ID and groaned.

"Hello, Ron."

"Ian, sorry to call you at home, but my doughnut costume seems to have run off."

"Sorry, Ron. A mistake. I'll bring it back."

"You're not on the schedule until Monday."

"No, sorry, Ron. And I'm out of town this weekend. Family stuff. Very sorry."

"I can't let anything happen to the doughnut, Ian–"

"No, Ron."

"–because I just don't want–"

"Mmm-hmm."

"—to have to explain to my regional manager why we need a new suit just nine months—*nine months*—after they sent us the last one."

"Yes, Ron."

"That'd look bad, Ian. Very bad."

"Yes, Ron."

"I don't like to look bad to the regional manager, Ian."

"Okay, Ron."

"So you won't let anything happen to it, right?"

"Right, Ron."

"Great."

There was an awkward pause. Ian began to wipe the chocolate from the doughnut with a T-shirt, but it only seemed to press the stain deeper into the foam.

"So, see you Monday morning, Ian."

"Right."

"With the suit."

"Definitely."

"Oh, one more thing, Ian. A woman stopped by the shop to say that she and her three-year-old had seen a large doughnut cursing in the parking lot. You wouldn't know anything about that, would you?"

"Um . . . sorry, Ron. 'Bye, Ron."

Ian set the Toady down on his dresser. He lifted the doughnut over his head, set it atop his mound of dirty clothes, and turned on his laptop. He sat on the edge of his bed and pecked out a quick reply to Danielle.

To: dmorrison@scsu.edu
From: ilafferty@toady.com
Subject: Re: Re: Re: road trip?

Okay, Miss Tasty. I'm there. Late Friday. I've
got your number.

Ian

Yeah, that's it. Say little, he thought. *Less is definitely more.*

He found driving directions to Danielle's sorority house online—
she was a Sigma Tau Delta, whatever that meant—and printed them.
He began to plot an itinerary and allowed himself to daydream about
their impending encounter. Sex. She'd pretty much promised to have
sex with him. His heart pounded. It wasn't just that he *wanted* experience with girls because, well, what heterosexual teenage boy didn't? It
was something more than that. Ian's own lack of experience with
women had made him feel like somewhat of a freak. His peers—even
his geekiest, most awkward peers—seemed to be participating in at least
some amount of romantic interaction, while he was having none. He
felt left out. He felt exiled on the wrong side of puberty. But now it
seemed that he was going to take a quantum sexual leap. He put the
laptop on the floor and stretched out on his bed. He wished for a moment that he could discuss his plan with Felicia, though he knew she'd
be indignant. She had always been a sort of moral compass for him.
He dissected the merits and risks of all social engagements with her.
But this particular one? No way. What good could possibly come

from the conversation? None. Was this more guilt that Ian was feeling? Maybe.

Felicia eventually called his house that night. But when the phone rang, Ian had been asleep for three hours.

When Ian blinked open his eyes, his room was full of sunlight. The digital clock beside his bed said 9:48.

It took him a few moments to process these key details:

1) He had not merely napped but had slept through the night.
2) His parents had neglected to wake him when they'd left for the airport.
3) He was already way behind schedule if he was going to reach Charleston by midnight. And . . .
4) *Felicia and Lance will be here in, like, ten minutes! Um . . . shit!*

He leaped out of bed and threw a change of clothes in a backpack, then grabbed the directions, his Toady, car keys, and wallet. He dragged the foam doughnut along with him, just in case he had to drive directly to work on Monday. Then he hurriedly showered, brushed his teeth, and got dressed in a plain T-shirt and cargo shorts.

His digital clock said 9:56. He raced for the front door.

When he opened it, Felicia Alpine was already striding up the Laffertys' front walk, smiling. She hugged Ian before he could say her name, and—despite the fact that he was in the midst of a frenetic near-escape—he was thrilled to see her. She had a postvacation glow at the edges of her otherwise familiar appearance. Her brown hair was bunched in asymmetric pigtails; she wore tattered jeans with a small bright green T-shirt that read JOLEY'S PANCAKE SILO, over a picture of a guy looking confused standing on top of a very tall stack of pancakes. She kissed Ian's cheeks, startling him.

"I have been in Europe, Monsieur Lafferty. *Zees* is how we say hello."

"Well, hello." He smiled and looked over her shoulder. "Um, Lance . . . you can just say hi. We won't kiss. Hope that's cool."

Lance exited the tiny Mazda and began to walk toward Ian, but Ian whooshed past him. He opened the Creature's trunk, tossing in his backpack and the doughnut.

"Nice to see that you're ready to go. I thought you were waffling a little yesterday, maybe wussing out."

Ian said nothing. He had hoped to avoid precisely this situation. He was struggling to come up with an acceptable reason to skip out on Lance-a-Palooza when Felicia grabbed his arm.

"Were you really asleep last night when I called? That's what your mom said. She's so worried about letting her li'l boy go into the big, bad city. . . ." Felicia pinched Ian's cheeks "But I promised her we'd protect you."

"Yeah." He grinned. "I was asleep. Pretty much a loser, I know. It's been nothing but work and video games. Maybe the occasional sitcom. It wears you out after a while. Sorry."

"Don't worry about it, kid. We've got the whole weekend to catch up. I have a lot to tell you." She squeezed his hand.

"Yeah," he said, looking toward Lance. "About this weekend . . ." He paused, paralyzed by total icy embarrassment. "I can't. I've got . . ."

He looked down at the Creature, which he'd bought from his grandmother's nursing home roommate, Norma, the previous year.

"It's my grandmother. She's not well. At all. Very sick. My parents are already down there. They left last night. Got a late phone call. Could be serious. I really have to go." He became instantly aware of his tendency to babble when nervous. Not that he could control it. "Sick, sick, sick. It's important that I go. Very big deal."

Ian glanced at Felicia, then quickly looked away. She seemed crestfallen and confused. He cringed. These were, after all, his oldest and closest friends. He looked again toward Lance.

"I'm sorry. I really can't. I wish I could. But I can't."

He climbed into the driver's side of the Creature.

"And you have to leave right now?" Felicia said.

"Yeah, I'm so late. I'll catch up on Monday. Really sorry."

Ian pulled out of the driveway quickly, still feeling awful. Felicia and Lance stood on the Laffertys' lawn, near the sprinkler, perplexed and looking at each other.

As bad as that moment had been—what with the lying and the

false debilitation of his poor, loving grandma—it would have been far worse telling them the full truth about Danielle, thought Ian.

He felt certain that as soon as he hit the highway he would begin to focus fully on the life-altering benefits of the trip ahead. But first he really needed to stop at a drugstore.

Ian parked the Creature in the Walgreens lot and entered the pharmacy, triggering an electronic chime. He dipped his head low, wishing that he could—just for the duration of this particular shopping trip—be completely invisible. Or at least well camouflaged. Instead, he had never felt more conspicuous. Of course, he had never been shopping for condoms.

The first challenge was to actually locate them without asking anyone for assistance: "Pardon me, ma'am, I was wondering if you could tell me where I might find the condoms? You know, um . . . for inhibiting the transfer of sperm and disease during sex?" No, that conversation wasn't happening.

He grabbed a plastic shopping basket. The thought of rushing into Walgreens, quickly slapping down a wad of cash for a box of condoms, then breathlessly rushing out seemed, well . . . icky. He would buy more than just condoms. He'd do some shopping for the trip.

Pick up some needed toiletries. Perhaps a magazine. Snacks for the road. Maybe a map.

He strolled through the aisles at a measured pace, flipping items into the basket. Sunglasses. Mouthwash. Disposable camera. A bag of Swedish fish. Four PayDay candy bars. An adhesive-backed dashboard compass. A travel-size bottle of Pert. The September issue of *PC Gamer*. A jar of chunky peanut butter. Plastic cutlery. A six-pack of Mountain Dew. A package of Twizzlers. Six Hostess fruit pies—two cherry, two peach, one blueberry, one apple. Floral-print napkins. A large atlas. Two giant bags of Doritos. A sleeve of Twinkies. A tube of Pringles.

But, after several minutes, still no condoms.

Ian began to sweat, and not just a little. Big drops beaded on his forehead and chest. He hoped the contraceptive selection process would be simple but began to fear that it wouldn't. He passed by racks of vitamins, cold remedies, pain relievers, lawn-care products, wind chimes, greeting cards, a giant bin of rubber balls.

But still no condoms.

Then he came upon a variety of feminine hygiene products and home pregnancy tests. *Birthy stuff,* he thought. *I must be getting close.*

Indeed he was. At the far end of the store, near the pharmacy's drop-off counter, Ian found the answers to his contraceptive needs. Far too many answers, in fact. He stared at the condom display as if it were a vast wall of hieroglyphics he'd been asked to decipher. He was overwhelmed by the variety of styles and features.

Ultrathin?

Large? Extra-large? XXL?

Ribbed? "For her pleasure!" the package claimed. *That seems thoughtful.*

Studded texture? *That seems a little sadistic.*

Glow-in-the-dark? *Are women aroused by the appearance of erectile radioactivity? Unlikely.*

An old, gray, grandmotherly looking woman carrying a giant purse shuffled by. She stared rather sourly at Ian as he examined the array of condoms. He blushed. A pair of young girls—neither could have been older than fourteen—trailed along behind her. While passing Ian, they quietly stared at their flip-flops. When they reached the next aisle, however, they began giggling. The laughter sent a wave of anxiety through Ian, as if he'd just been depantsed in his school cafeteria.

He lunged at the display, grabbing a random package without caring which odd style he'd selected. He placed the condoms at the bottom of his basket, underneath his magazine, where he hoped they would cause him no further shame.

That's it. Almost over.

Part of him wanted to simply bolt for the checkout line, but Ian reasoned that he should maintain his deliberate pace.

Draw no attention. Stay cool. Relax. This is easy. Like shopping for socks.

He continued toward the pharmacy drop-off, which he intended to pass with a nonchalant gait before heading to the front register and, ultimately, the exit.

A female pharmacist glanced up from a plastic tub of medicine as he approached. She was blond, twentysomething, deeply tan—almost unnaturally good looking for a health care professional, Ian thought.

And waaaaay too good looking for Ian to interact with while buying condoms. She smiled at him. Ian was horrified. She seemed vaguely familiar. He turned away suddenly, nearly spinning on his heels. *That was probably a little awkwar*d, he thought. But he couldn't look back. *Pretend you forgot something.*

"Ohh . . ." he said, raising his hand to his head, hoping to convey the impression that he'd neglected to grab something terribly important and located nowhere near the pharmacy. He felt the perspiration on his thin face. *C'mon. You're just a guy out shopping, that's all you are. Ho-hum. Just out picking up a few things. Just chill.* He walked with haste away from the pharmacist and toward the checkout line.

But the checkout line was at a standstill. Ian stopped thirty feet from the register, near a bin stuffed with $4.99 DVDs. He feigned interest in *Quigley Down Under* so as to avoid the crowd. The employee at the register wasn't moving, and neither were the many frowning customers waiting in her line. The checkout girl sighed, then jabbed her finger at the number pad on a telephone and spoke into the receiver. Her flat voice carried throughout the store.

"Manager to the front, please. I need an override. Customers waiting. Manager . . ."

A few shoppers groaned. They shifted their feet. Ian scanned the store, seeing no other open lanes. The store seemed bereft of useful employees. Reluctantly, he took a step toward the line when he noticed the two young gigglers at its end, smirking behind their grandmother. Ian presumed they'd noticed him—Condom Boy—and were making wisecracks under their breath. He froze. He couldn't possibly join the unmoving line directly behind two girls who were openly ridiculing him. No, he needed distance between himself and the gigglers. He needed . . .

"Attention, customers, no waiting in the pharmacy," said an incorporeal voice. "Please bring your purchases to the pharmacy. No waiting."

Good grief. Do I buy condoms from the abnormally hot pharmacist, or suffer further taunting by a pair of annoying junior-high chicks?

Customers began to leave the checkout line, drifting toward the pharmacy. The two girls, however, waited like toy poodles beside the old woman. Ian left the bin of movies, dropping *Quigley* atop the pile, and marched again toward the rear of the store. He would take his chances with the fetching pharmacist.

He made eye contact with her just as he passed the pregnancy tests, and she again grinned at him. He reached the pharmacy checkout just ahead of the pack of other impatient shoppers. The pharmacist—her name tag read BETSY—smiled brighter as he began to empty his basket. Ian nodded at her, returning the smile sheepishly.

The pharmacist chuckled. Ian was aghast.

He set the Pringles on the counter, and the tube rolled softly toward her. She stopped it with an index finger.

"Hey, you," she chirped.

Wha—? Is she flirting? Good God, she's a pharmacist! That's, like, half a doctor! I mean, if I were going to date a pharmacist, this would be the best-case scenario. No question. But girls my own age don't even flirt with me. And anyway, pharmacists don't flirt, they golf. And they commiserate with old people about medical conditions. But they certainly don't flirt. So what the heck is happening here?

"Um . . . hello," Ian offered. The pharmacist laughed again, leaning closer. He placed the Mountain Dew on the counter with a thud.

"You don't recognize me, do you?"

"You're, um . . . well, you're a very helpful pharmacist. And I'm sure a very good one."

"Ian Lafferty, you doofus. You crack me up."

"Doofus"? I haven't been called a doofus since—

She took his right hand in hers and said, "It's me, Betsy." She waited, looking for a hint of recognition on the bewildered boy's face. "Betsy McNaughton? Helloooo, I was only your babysitter for, like, six years."

She hugged him over his pile of road-trip supplies.

Ian felt a sudden wave of total familiarity, followed by a warm sense of reunion—the smokin' hot pharmacist draped around his neck was, in fact, easily the most entertaining babysitter of his childhood—followed soon after by a wave of abject terror. This was *definitely* not the person from whom he wanted to purchase his condoms. No, not at all.

"So, how are you, Ian?" she asked, helping him unload his basket. "And how are your parents? My God, I haven't seen you in forever. What's up? Obviously I went to pharmacy school, and you . . . Hmm, you must be a senior now, right? Maybe in college already?"

He barely shrugged. She paused, looking at him and shaking her head lightly.

"Wow, Ian Lafferty!"

She said his name as if he were a nearly forgotten celebrity who'd stumbled into her store. Like "Wow, Corey Haim!"

This can't be happening. He swatted at his pile of fruit pies, hoping to unearth the condoms and get them out of sight before Betsy reached them.

"Hey, Ian, do you remember when we invented the Lafferty pentathlon?" She grinned, plucking a bag of Doritos from the basket and scanning it at her register. "What was it? Let's see . . . tetherball, Scrabble, thumb-wrestling, Mortal Kombat on . . . oh, what game system? Nintendo? And what else? What was the fifth thing?"

"Hungry Hungry Hippos," Ian said, panicking.

Condoms, condoms, condoms . . . Where the F are the damn condoms?!

"That's right!" Betsy exclaimed. "Hungry Hippos was the fifth. The Lafferty pentathlon was 'the ultimate test of skill across five disciplines'!" She laughed and smiled. "You were a hoot, Ian! You were just the cutest little boy, I swear. And do you remember the time that we thought your cat had fallen into the neighbor's pool and couldn't get himself ou–?"

She stopped in midword, eyeing the item in her hand. Ian eyed it, too. It was a three-pack of neon orange, mango-flavored condoms. The package had fluorescent yellow script that began, *Once she tastes the tropics . . .*

Betsy's eyes widened. She dropped the package onto the counter, scanned it quickly–without touching it–and flicked it into a plastic Walgreens shopping bag as if she were disposing of an animal turd. She smirked. Ian quickly emptied the remaining items from his basket.

"So, um . . . yeah, that was a wacky cat," said Betsy, attempting to compose herself. "Good times."

She was no longer looking at him. Apparently, Ian detected, she was no longer feeling nostalgic, either. Just amused. She quickly scanned and bagged the last few items in Ian's basket. He said nothing. She was evidently fighting a laugh.

"That's $59.89, *Mister* Lafferty," said Betsy.

Ian handed her three twenty-dollar bills, feeling unbelievably self-conscious and weirdly apologetic.

"So, Betsy. Really nice to see you." He offered a sort of half-wave.

She raised her eyebrows, then blinked her eyes and offered a broad smile.

"'Bye, Ian. Nice to see you, too." She handed him a penny and a dime. "Have a great weekend." She gestured toward the bags. "I mean, you seem to have, uh . . . exciting plans."

Ian smiled a painful smile, mumbled, "Thanks, Betsy," and fled.

Oh, that sucked, he thought. *Yup, that sure sucked. That sucked, it sucked. Itsuckeditsuckeditsuckeditsucked. Ugh. Pull it together, Ian. Priorities. You have your condoms. They're a little wacky, true. But they'll probably work. If the lights are off. Unless they glow, in which case I'll look like a traffic flare.* He exhaled audibly. *Aargh. Itsuckeditsuckeditsucked . . .*

Ian stopped at the ATM by the main entrance and withdrew three hundred dollars for gas, food, and incidentals en route. At a wage of $8.35 an hour, he calculated, those three hundred bucks represented basically a full week of menial, doughnut-related work. He winced involuntarily.

He exited Walgreens through the automatic door and emerged into the warm, bright Friday sun. He breathed deeply and gave his head a shake, as if sloughing off his panic. He stepped slowly toward the Creature, staring at the black asphalt and hoping to clear his head. His bags swung at his side.

"Would you like some help to your car, sir," called a cheerful voice from just ahead—a cheerful voice that was not supposed to be there. "That's a lotta bags for a skinny dude like you to carry all the way to this ginormous yellow car."

Ian froze.

Lance was sitting on the hood of the Creature, dangling his feet. Felicia sat beside him, waving happily.

Oh, fudge.

Ian thought he had already extracted himself from this predicament. He stared at his friends and his shoulders sagged. He forced a grin.

"Are we just completely freaking you out, Ian?" said Felicia. "We're like stalkers, yeah?" She launched herself off the car and bounded toward him across the asphalt.

"A little. Maybe." He paused. "No, I mean. Not really. What's, um . . . what's up?"

Lance hopped off the hood.

"We're giving you another chance to partake of the wanton splendor that will be Lance-a-Palooza."

"'Wanton'?" Ian asked. "Last year we sat around for, like, six hours while Doug got high, watching *Pee-Wee's Big Adventure*."

"Dude, that was just one night. And remember how completely *toasted* my cousin was? C'mon, he was kind of funny."

"He made me sad."

"Well, you know what makes *me* sad? You bailing on us this year. For what? Your grandma? It was your grandma, right? You're such a crappy liar, Ian."

"She's sick. She's very old. In a home. They puree her food. It's sad. I really can't get out of it."

"C'mon, Ian," pleaded Felicia, gripping his hand. "We haven't seen each other in soooo long. I'll regale you with stories of my adventures along the Mediterranean coast." She took a step back. "They're exciting stories, I promise. I danced in clubs. I drank sangria. I walked topless on beaches. I met mysterious boys who spoke no English—I engaged in intimate cultural exchanges with them."

"Sounds like fluid exchanges," snorted Lance.

"Cultural intersections take many forms," she said.

Ian didn't enjoy the act of deceiving Felicia. Not at all. But he dreaded the thought of telling her the truth about his weekend plans even more.

"Look, I wish I could go. I do. But I can't." He trudged toward his car with his head bent low. He set his Walgreens bags down as he unlocked the driver's side door of the Creature. Lance picked up a bag and began rifling through the contents.

"Dude, this is a lotta stuff to take to Grandma's. Is it all for you? Is it for her?"

"Hey, put that down!" yelped Ian.

Lance was undeterred. He walked around to the passenger side of the car with Ian following behind.

"Holy crapballs!" said Lance, digging in the bag. Ian cringed. *No, please, God, no. I don't need this. Not now, not today . . .*

Lance held up a pair of fruit pies.

"You've cornered the market on Hostess fruit pies! Does your grandmother have scurvy?"

Ian felt momentarily relieved, though he was still anxious to get the bag out of Lance's hands. He snatched the pies and said, "Gimme the bag, Lance!"

"All right, chill," said Lance, returning the supplies. "I guess if you say you've gotta do the family thing this weekend, Felicia and I can go to Doug's without you. But she might cramp my style. Other girls might think we're, like, together. That's why I needed you around, du—"

"No . . . *way*!" exclaimed Felicia.

Ian spun around to see her mouth agape, her eyes glued to the contents of another Walgreens bag. His pulse accelerated; his head seemed to spin. Felicia continued stammering. "No . . . freakin' . . . *way*. No. Way. Nuh-uh."

"What?" asked Lance.

"I can't even tell you," said Felicia. She spoke to Lance but stared at Ian with a puzzled expression. "Seriously. I can't tell you. I can't verbalize it. There are no words. Check this out."

With the slightest flip of her wrist, Felicia sent a small black box out of the bag and into the air with a high arc. It sailed over the car, tumbling well above Ian—he read the letters on the box as it passed overhead: *M-A-N-G-O P-A-S-S-I-O-N*—and landed with a slap against the asphalt a few feet beyond Lance. Ian took a half-step toward the box, but Lance quickly grabbed it.

So endeth the lie, Ian thought.

"You . . . are . . . *shitting* me!" said Lance. He cackled. "Did you buy these on purpose? They must be having a giveaway, right? Like a free trial of fruit-flavored condoms if you purchase a half-dozen fruit pies? 'Cause no way does Ian Lafferty . . ."

". . . buy neon condoms," said Felicia, looking appalled. "Or any other kind of condom," she added. "I thought you said you had a boring summer, Ian. Doughnuts, video games, TV—that sort of thing."

"They're not, um . . . It's nothing. They're not really, um . . ."

"They're not *what*, dude?" asked Lance. "They're not for you? Are they for *Grandma*? Or maybe you're hoping to nail a few ninety-year-old hotties at the nursing home?"

Ian seemed to shrink. He couldn't continue lying to his friends. What could he possibly say? He tried the truth. Or at least some of the truth.

"I'm not really going to visit my grandmother," he said.

"No kidding, Ian," said Felicia. "We appreciate your openness."

"Sorry. I just . . . I wasn't all that sure how to tell you guys. . . . It's a little weird, I mean. . . ."

"What the hell, Lafferty?" Felicia demanded. "You've got enough shit in these bags to stock a 7-Eleven. And you have maps. And birth control. Are you dropping out of school to become some kind of traveling sex freak?"

"Cool," said Lance. "I'd do that. If you want a partner—a partner while traveling, I mean. Not while having sex."

"Shut up, Lance," said Felicia, still looking at Ian.

"We could wear capes," continued Lance. "And masks. And tight costumes with big belts. And we'd have names like 'the Mango Ranger' and—"

"Look, I should've been totally honest with you. Really, I should have. But it's a little embarrassing." Ian paused. "No, it's completely embarrassing."

"*What?*" asked Felicia and Lance in unison.

Ian cleared his throat, then moved his hands as if speaking. But no words came. He considered different ways to phrase the truth, finally arriving at this: "A girl has agreed to have sex with me."

"Well, we figured you were probably having sex with *something,* based on the contents of this box," said Lance, waving the condoms.

"A girl 'has agreed to have sex' with you?" said Felicia, her fingers hooking the quotes in the air. "Is that right?"

"That's it," answered Ian.

"Do I know this person?" Lance asked. "Is it that Amanda chick from your dad's office? She's just a sophomore. And she's all into, like, goth stuff. Very weird. Still, very cute. Don't take her across state lines, though. Federal crime. Bad news."

"No, it's not Amanda. It's nobody you kno—"

"It's not Miss Destri, is it? The physics teacher? So gross. But I can't deny she's hot. There's this whole phenomenon—I was reading about it the other day—where creepy young teachers try to scam on teen—"

"No. And *ick.* No. It's nobody you guys know."

"You're not paying this person, right?" continued Lance. "Because sometimes even if you don't think you're paying them, they ask for money when it's over. And then you're in trouble. I saw this thing on HBO where this guy—"

"Um, no," said Ian, smiling in spite of himself. "I'm not paying anyone."

"So is it like a mail-order-bride thing?" asked Lance. "My uncle Lou just told the family he was getting married to some girl named Pelagia. She's Ukrainian. My dad was like, 'How'd you meet a Ukrainian? You live in Wisconsin. On a farm.' My uncle's like, 'We were pen pals.' Pen pals! Total mail-order-bride situation. Now I'm going to have a mail-order aunt. And you're going to have a mail-order sex partn—"

"No, I will not have a mail-order anything." Ian shifted uncomfortably. "But you're getting warmer."

"I'm getting warmer? Seriously? I really don't get it. She's Ukrainian?"

"No. Now you're colder. Well, I dunno. I mean, she could be Ukrainian. I don't know. We haven't met. In person."

"How *have* you met?" Felicia asked.

"Online. On the Internet. Chatting."

Felicia shook her head.

"Sweet!" said Lance.

"Who *does* this?" Felicia asked. "Who just meets some skank on the Internet and has sex with her? *Sex!*"

"She's not a ska—" began Ian.

"I seriously can't believe this is happening."

"She's not a skank, Felicia."

"Oh, she's a sweet little churchgoing farm girl who meets men on MySpace and agrees to have sex with them? Really? How lovely."

"It's not like that."

"Ian, you were a member of the Boy Scouts, like, two years ago," Felicia said, wrapping her arms around her waist.

"He's getting a skank badge," Lance said, not quite under his breath.

"Okay, stop it," said Ian, leaning against his car. "And I was not a very active Boy Scout. This discussion is not going well."

"Dude!" said Lance. "It's going very well. This is awesome."

"This discussion is a lot of things," said Felicia. "Bizarre. Depraved. Chilling. Ethically bankrupt. But it is *not* awesome."

"Maybe I could explain things a little better," offered Ian.

"We're listening," Felicia shot back.

Ian began describing his courtship with Danielle, selecting the details carefully. He portrayed their relationship as something that had evolved slowly, naturally, and sweetly (when in fact it had evolved in a week, largely through deception, and mostly because Ian had been a complete sphincter). Still, Ian gushed to his friends about all the good qualities he could only hope Danielle possessed. Felicia paced, visibly agitated. Lance occasionally interjected with, "Get to the part where you demand sex!" Ian ignored him.

"Fine, Ian," Felicia said at last. "She sounds sweet. For a girl who seduces guys online, very sweet. But how—and why—did you agree to have sex with her? How did you even introduce the subject? And where will it happen? Are you traveling to South Carolina for this— 'Hey, Dad, I'm gonna go screw this girl I met on the Internet. Can I take the car?'—or is she driving here? Are you meeting at a neutral site? And how will—?"

"Okay, okay. That's a lot of stuff to answer," Ian said, waving his arms. "First of all, she invited me to stay with her at school." Ian showed Danielle's most recent message to his friends. Felicia and Lance exchanged astonished looks. "The sex is implied in the invitation, I think."

"Well, not necess—" began Felicia, before Lance interrupted.

"Hell, yeah! Of course the sex is implied! What, you're supposed to get in your car and drive across the country to go see her so that you can take her to dinner? No. No, no, no. The sex is definitely implied. Good man, Ian. Good man."

"So yeah, I'm going to Charleston. Like, right now. I've never been, but I have maps. My parents just think I'm with you guys."

"They think you're with *us*?" asked Felicia, horrified by the idea of covering for Ian under such circumstances. "That's a little dangerous, don't you think? You were conning us too, Ian. How were we supposed to cover for you?"

"The plan could've been formulated a bit better, it's true. But the important thing was to get on the road. That's all I was thinking about, really. It's all I'm thinking about right now, actually. Even talking about this now is costing me time."

"And sex acts," said Lance.

"Look, I've really gotta go," said Ian.

"Sweet!" said Lance. "We'll come with! It's a little radical, a little reckless. Let's go. We'll road trip for Lance-a-Palooza. There aren't many things I'd drive halfway across the country in your car to do, but this is definitely one of them. If we leave Ian Lafferty's virginity in South Carolina, it's totally worth it."

"You want to *help* him do this?" asked Felicia indignantly. "This is so completely wrong. This is *not* how it's supposed to be, Ian. Do you love her? Shouldn't you at least *love* her? Don't you think the first time you have sex should be special? Shouldn't it be memorable?"

"You mean with candles around the tub?" asked Lance. "And Justin Timberlake songs?"

"No. Just special. Because of the person you're with. This is so . . . so . . . planned. And so casual. This is like a meeting of the varsity sex club. It's wrong."

"Ooooh, I would like that club," said Lance. "We could wear little fig leaves for the yearbook picture. We could—"

"Don't be glib. Ian is making a gigantic mistake here."

"Let me see your map, dude," Lance said to Ian. "If we go through Memphis, we can maybe stop at Graceland."

"Lance, we're driving me to go have sex. We're not stopping at tourist attractions. We're hauling ass, and we're taking a direct route. And . . . oh, what the hell am I even saying? This is a solitary mission. I work alone. You can't come."

"Of course we can! We're your best friends. You need us now more than ever. And I think Memphis is totally on the way. If we're taking the Creature, which we better, 'cause we sure aren't taking the Mazda, then we need to—"

Felicia erupted. "I cannot believe I'm listening to this, this, this . . . *bullshit!*"

Ian and Lance were startled. Felicia, normally composed at all times, was clearly flustered. She glared hard at Ian. He shrank against the Creature.

"Don't be like that, Felicia," said Lance. "The boy needs support.

And if you come along, that's potentially two votes to one in favor of the occasional roadside attraction. Plus you'll have several hours to try to talk Ian off the ledge of sexual promiscuity. Save his soul, et cetera."

Felicia closed her eyes, bent her head, and linked her hands behind her neck.

Oh God, Ian thought. *I can't just drive off with her stuck in this disappointed-in-Ian-Lafferty pose.*

"I suppose the embarrassment I was trying to spare myself is already, um . . . embarrassing me," he said. "So come on, Felicia. Come with. Maybe I need the company. I certainly don't need Lance in my ear for fifteen hours."

"This is so not you, Ian."

"I've been totally inert this summer, Felicia. You guys have been away doing fabulous things, and I've just been getting up at dawn and going to the mall. Now there are only a few days left for me to salvage a little excitement from a completely wasted summer."

Ian thrust a peach fruit pie toward her.

"I have snacks."

She didn't quite laugh.

"Oh, c'mon. I really just . . . I *need* this trip, Felicia. If I'm going to go through with it—and I'll admit, on the surface, it might seem like a questionable decision—then maybe I'd like some discussion on the way. Dissenting viewpoints are welcome. I saved loads of money this summer, what with working all the time and not having a thing to do, so I'll buy the food and gas. And we can listen to your music. There's cool stuff to see along the way, I think—it's a big tourist city, Charleston. Old houses, pirates, pretty buildings, that sort of thing."

Felicia exhaled audibly. She gave Ian a cold look. He felt his stomach tighten. He hated—*hated*—seeing Felicia upset.

"C'mon, Felicia," he pleaded, gripping her elbow. "Please come have sex with me."

She raised her eyebrows.

"Um, what I mean is—"

"Easy there, tiger," said Lance. "You should probably take the girls one at a time when you're just starting out."

Ian lowered his head. "That was poorly worded. But I think you know what I mean."

Felicia softened. She looked toward Lance.

"Keys," she said flatly.

Lance tossed her the keys to his car.

"Just let me get my bag, Ian. And, if you can spare another minute from your tight schedule, I'd like to pop into Walgreens for some food that wasn't made by Hostess or doesn't end in *-eetos*. You really do eat like shit for the son of a dentist, Ian."

He smiled.

"Wait up," said Lance, beginning to jog toward the store entrance. "If *I'm* going to some Southern college town, we should probably bring more than three condoms."

"Creep," said Felicia.

"Let's just get a few things clear," said Ian, accelerating onto Interstate 88 in the early afternoon. "This trip has rules. And it has a schedule. And it has a map."

Ian glanced at Felicia, who sat in the passenger seat, then swiveled around to emphasize his point to Lance.

"Thou shalt not deviate from the rules, the schedule, or the map."

"Okay, Moses," said Lance. "Whatever. So no Graceland?"

"I'm serious," said Ian. "I'm completely, totally, deadly serious. In three days, we have to travel 1,870 miles across parts of six states in a car that's older than me. The first 935 miles of our trip are really the most time-sensitive. We only stop for gas. There will be no stopping to drink or eat or pee. On the return trip—if our mission has been a success—I might indulge you. Operative word: *might*. I have to be at work by six-thirty on Monday. And I'm pretty sure I can't be late."

"Um . . . I can't pee?" asked Felicia.

"We pee in pop cans," said Ian jauntily. A small plastic hula girl jiggled atop the dashboard.

"I don't pee in pop cans, Ian. I pee in toilets. Private toilets that have been recently cleaned and smell like pine needles. I do not pee in cars, nor into cans. I'm not an exhibitionist, and I can't pee for accuracy."

"Okay, you make a fine point. Felicia gets three pee stops in addition to our regular stops for gas. But try to limit your liquid intake. And you can't use two pee stops in the same state." He paused. "Lance, you still pee in pop cans."

"What if I have more than twelve ounces of peeing to do, Ian?"

"This is just vile," said Felicia.

"You use two cans. And you make the switch quickly."

"Really, this is too gross."

"Dude, you don't even have cup holders. Where do the pee cans go?"

"Dump them out the window. But we're not slowing down, so be careful not to let it blow back in—"

"Seriously, stop!" Felicia said. "This is beyond gross. This is, like, medieval. Drop me off on the side of the road. I'll hitchhike back."

"Ian, don't stress about time. You're in with this girl. *In.* She won't turn you away just because you're not punctual. Anyway, you have bigger worries than what time you get there."

"Like what, exactly?"

"Ian," began Lance, hoisting himself up toward the front seat, "how much sex have you had exactly?"

Ian said nothing.

"Well?" Lance said, waiting to hear an answer that he already knew.

"What's your point?"

"And how many condoms have you used? No, how many condoms have you ever actually *seen*? You need a tutorial, dude, or you'll look like an amateur."

"I *am* an amateur. If you're a professional, I'm pretty sure that you're breaking the law."

"Well, you know what I mean. You'll look like a rookie. A little too innocent. Girls don't think it's sexy when a guy can't subtly apply the condom. I'm right about this, aren't I, Felicia?"

"Can we talk about peeing again?" she asked.

"Nope. It's time for Ian to learn a few things."

Lance tore through the Walgreens bags until he found the package of Twizzlers. He quickly ripped the bag open with his teeth, then peeled off a single Twizzler. He pulled it taut, pinching each end between a thumb and index finger, and held it directly between Ian and Felicia.

"Let's say this Twizzler is Ian's, um . . . Do you have a name for it, dude?"

Ian took his eyes from the road to quickly examine the length of red licorice. "Is that supposed to be my . . . thing?"

"So that's what you call it? Just 'thing'? How scary."

"*No!* That's not what I call it." He paused. "I mean, I don't call it anything."

"Whatever. Just trying to make you feel more comfortable with the demonstration."

"You could make me feel more comfortable," said Felicia, "by shutting the heck up. And by demonstrating *nothing*. Good God, this is obscene."

"No," said Lance. "This is a public service announcement." He removed a hand from the Twizzler, allowing it to bend and droop. "Let's just say this rather sad and flaccid little fella is Ian's 'thing,' as he calls it."

Lance reached into his back pocket and removed his wallet, from which he then extracted a wrapped condom.

"Felicia, will you be so kind as to hold Ian's thing while I unwrap this condom?"

He thrust the Twizzler toward her.

"Um . . . no. No, I will not."

"Just take it, prude," said Lance, dropping the Twizzler into her lap.

She jumped, not quite squealing. Ian was paying a good deal of attention to Lance.

"You keep a condom in your wallet? Like, all the time?"

"Dude, you never know. Or at least that's what you're trying to convey to girls—with *this* guy, you never know. Anything's possible. He carries a condom, just in case."

"Hmm," grunted Ian.

"It's very important, by the way, that you keep your mango mojo in your wallet," said Lance. "If it's in the front pocket, you'll look too eager. Too desperate. The wallet is best. If it's in the wallet, Danielle will just think . . ."

" . . . with *me*, anything's possible," finished Ian.

"Exactly. Like this sort of thing is always happening to you."

"Good God, Ian," said Felicia. "You're becoming a little Lance replicant. Mini-Lance. Not good, Ian. Not good."

Lance quickly unwrapped the condom. Then he snatched back the Twizzler from Felicia.

"It's like this, Ian." He pressed an end of the Twizzler into the flat disc of the condom, then unrolled the latex to cover the licorice. "Very simple, really. Do it quickly." He flapped the encased Twizzler in Ian's face. "Or you can let the girl do it, in which case there's no need to hurry. But that's kind of a bold move."

"Enough!" said Felicia. She swatted the condom/Twizzler combo from Lance's hand onto the floor of the Creature. "New topic, okay? Or no topic at all. Can we just not have any sex-ed lessons for a while?"

Ian, embarrassed, said nothing. Lance, unabashed, spoke up.

"But, Felicia, we were really hoping you'd show us how to . . ."

She glared at Lance and raised her hand in a display of mock violence.

"You don't wanna taste the Alpine backhand, Lance. You're very close. And anyway, I'm sure there's nothing I can show you that you haven't already mastered, right?"

"You're too kind."

With that, the car fell quiet. Felicia soon slept, beginning to erase her jet lag. She curled herself into a ball against the Creature's vinyl seat. Lance flipped through *PC Gamer,* occasionally ridiculing the magazine's audience. He called Doug to reveal that they'd canceled their Lance-a-Palooza plans. Doug responded with, "Oh, that's cool. Wait, you were coming to see me? When? For what?"

Ian drove.

He drove through the staid suburbs of Chicago, then inched past the imposing skyscrapers of the city in thick, frustrating midday traffic. He traveled east along Lake Michigan, by the refineries, steel mills, and other filth-spewing horrors of the I-80/94 industrial corridor. Then he plunged south on I-65 toward central Indiana, speeding past cornfields, pig farms, strip malls, highway oases, and bustling college towns. He also spent his time thinking. In particular, he thought about the possibility that he was going to look like a complete fool trying to have sex with a girl who—if she was willing to make herself so readily available to him—was almost certainly not a virgin. Ian, of course, wanted to seem sexually capable, despite the fact that a major reason he'd embarked on the trip was to *acquire* the beginnings of a sexual portfolio. And, of course, to get acquainted with Danielle. But especially to get acquainted with sex. He began to think that he might also be attempting to satisfy some less-than-conscious desire simply to do whatever it was that guys—typical all-American spitball-shooting, beer-guzzling, meathead guys—were supposed to want to do.

That'd kinda suck. I'm not like that, right? No. This trip is about excitement. Randomness. Uncertainty. Breaking out of Naperville. And who knows how things might go with Danielle? We might just have a little something.

On he drove, rarely stopping, making excellent time. Then Felicia woke up.

"Where are we?" she asked shakily, lifting her head for the first time in nearly three hours.

"About twenty-five minutes beyond Indianapolis," said Ian. He gestured over his shoulder. Felicia glanced back. The skyline of Indiana's capital was dominated by a single tower that seemed to rise from the dead center of the town. *Like the city is giving you the finger,* Ian had thought when they approached.

"Do we need to get gas anytime soon?" Felicia asked.

"Nope. Just stopped about an hour ago. You slept right through it."

"Well, then I think I need one of my pee stops."

"Can you wait just a little while?" asked Lance. "There's hardly any civilization out here."

"Uh . . . nope."

"Sweet!" Lance chirped sarcastically. "Yay for tiny bladders, then. How nice to see a bit more rural America."

"When nature calls, it calls, Lance."

After a few tense minutes—during which Felicia rapidly tapped the floor of the Creature with her bare feet—Ian found a relatively clean-looking Mobil station just off a highway exit. As he pulled up to a gas pump, Felicia bolted for the food mart entrance. She soon emerged with a bathroom key, then sprinted off behind the small store.

"The restroom must be around back," said Lance, drifting toward the food mart. "Guess I'll go, too, what with me having no pee breaks. That's so sexist."

"Sure. Cry me a river, Lance. Hurry up. *Hurry.*"

"Just feed the Creature, Ian."

Ian put another $6.82 of gas in his giant car, washed the bug splatter from its windows, and anxiously waited for his friends.

And waited. He sent Danielle a quick text:

Indiana, land of 1,000 od0rs.

And he waited some more. And waited, and waited.

At last, Felicia returned.

"Refreshed?" Ian asked.

"Yes, I am, thanks."

"*Please* get in the car," Ian pleaded.

Felicia shook her head and groaned. "Ian, I really need to talk to you. I think—"

"You think I'm making a huge mistake. I know. And I might be making a huge mistake. I can't disagree. But this summer, I've just been so . . . so . . . well, *nothing*. I've been nothing at all. I've done nothing of consequence. This trip at least feels adventurous, like I'm trying to experience something. I don't know. . . ."

"That's not actually what I need to talk to you about, Ian. I mean, it's a good topic. A very worthy topic. It's probably what I should be saying to you. But it's not what I'm trying to say." She paused, opening the Creature's door and sitting down. "It's like this: on my trip I had plenty of time to think abou—"

"See, *that's* the problem! You had this fabulous vacation. You saw God knows what, you ate God knows what, you met God knows who. And what did I do? Nothin'. Not a thing. I mean, I played Halo. And Halo 2. And Warcraft. And I sold doughnuts. That's *it*, Felicia. That's it." He looked away. "I need this trip to work out. Which means, right now, I have to get Lance to hurry up."

He marched off behind the store. Felicia sank into the seat.

Ian was practically sprinting when he arrived at the dented, half-rusted metal door behind the gas station marked BA HRO M in black magnetic letters. He rapped forcefully with his right fist.

"Come on! What are you doing in there? Napping? This is totally unbelievable. How much can you pee, anyway?"

Ian heard a flush, followed by the sound of running water.

"About time, asshat! Yeesh."

The door began to creak open.

"Seriously, man, what the he–?"

The person who emerged from the bathroom was not Lance.

It was, in fact, a man roughly the size of three Lances. His long beard, which hung down to his chest, contained bits of what seemed to be ground beef. He wore a torn sleeveless NASCAR T-shirt and a black trucker hat that said FAT BASTARD. A single word was tattooed on his left arm:

PIE

On his right arm was a tattoo of a skull, also wearing a trucker hat that said FAT BASTARD. On his neck, he had a tattoo of a zipper. He spoke in a low monotone.

"Were you addressing me?"

"Um . . . no," said Ian, backing away. "Well, I didn't know that you were *you*. I thought you were my friend."

"That wasn't very friendly, all those things you said." He paused. "You called me 'asshat.'"

"No, that wasn't friendly, you're right. It certainly was not. And I apologize for that comment. Sincerely. I'm sorry that you had to hear those things. It's just that, um . . . my friend, he just peed an hour ago. I thought . . . Well, it's not important what I thought. The important thing, I think, is that you take as long as you need. In there." Ian gestured toward the bathroom. "To pee. Or whatever."

The pair stared at each other in silence for a moment.

"It was thoughtless, those things I said," Ian offered.

The giant man approached Ian slowly, clapped his shoulder, and lumbered off toward the entrance of the food mart. From the other side of the small structure, Lance soon appeared. An attractive blonde walked beside him. Lance's right arm was draped over her shoulders. She seemed to have been recently crying.

"Hey, there you are, dude," said Lance. The girl at his side sniffed loudly. "I've been looking everywhere for you." Lance paused, then winked at his friend. "Hey, Ian, have you met Susie?"

"No, Lance. No, I have not met Susie." Ian took a breath and looked at his feet. "I haven't met a lot of people around here, really. What with all the driving. And not actually living anywhere near here."

Susie continued her sniffing. Her face was streaked with makeup. She was disarmingly attractive, in a perky, cheerleader sort of way. Her skin was almost freakishly tan, her hair was aggressively blond, and her clothes were negligible. She wore a midriff-baring pink top and a seemingly toddler-size denim skirt. Susie was clearly distraught.

"Well, let me introduce you," said Lance, smoothly. "Ian, this is Susie. She's a cashier here at the food mart. Susie, meet my good friend Ian."

"It's . . . (*sniff*) . . . it's really . . ." Susie wiped her cheeks with a tissue, removing a multicolored muck of makeup, tears, and eye goo. "It's really . . . (*snort*) . . . very nice to meet you, Ian."

She then collapsed into Lance's arms in a spasm of crying.

Ian felt his chest tighten. Lance softly massaged Susie's shoulders with his left hand and gave Ian a thumbs-up with the right. He mouthed the word *wow*.

Ian cleared his throat. A cold, pragmatic voice within Ian told him—no, it *urged* him—not to dally, not to waste any time attending to the problems of distraught girls. But a somewhat stronger voice within Ian—one that was somewhat more sympathetic—urged him to see what, if anything, could be done to help poor Susie.

"She needs a ride home," said Lance. Then, quietly in Susie's ear, "It's gonna be all right, Suze. Really. A smart, beautiful girl like you can do soooo much better."

"A ride home," repeated Ian. Susie turned to face him, pouting. "Where does she live? Where do you live, Susie? We could . . . I don't know—what's the problem? Is there someone we should call?" Susie sniffed.

A single tear fell down her face, disappearing when it hit her sparkly pink lip gloss. She again dabbed her eyes with the tissue.

"My . . . (*sniff*) . . . Rick, my boyfriend, he . . . (*snort*) . . . well, he usually gives me a ride . . . (*sniff*) . . . We had a fight an' now I don't think . . . (*sniff*) . . . well, he's not gonna pick me up today . . . (*snort*) . . . He probably won't pick me up ever again. We broke up. But I understand if you can't—"

"If we *can't* give you a ride?!" said Lance, as if offended by the implication. "*Can't?* That's just nonsense. Come on, let's get you to the car."

He led her by the arm toward the Creature. Ian trailed behind, a little bewildered and exceedingly anxious. *This could be fine. Maybe she*

lives near the interstate. She does seem very upset over this Rick. Better protect her from Lance, too, then get out of—oh, hell, I don't even know where we are. But it's not South Carolina.

As they neared the Creature, Ian caught sight of Felicia through the windshield. She was laughing, having just noticed the whimpering young thing on Lance's arm. This was a classic Lance pickup, after all. He could be adrift on an iceberg in the Arctic yet still manage to stumble across some hot, gullible young Inuit girl to seduce. Ian, on the other hand, felt as if he could be shipwrecked on a deserted island in the Pacific with a gaggle of female porn stars, yet only manage to become the nice geeky friend. He sighed as Lance helped Susie into the backseat.

"Hi, I'm Felicia!" chirped the very amused girl in the passenger seat. Lance gently shut the rear door. Ian grabbed his arm and spoke quietly, inches from Lance's face.

"There really isn't time for you to scam on any girls right now, Lance. You know that, right? If you'll recall, we were trying to get *me* to Charleston so that *I* can, well . . . do what you're trying to do with this poor unsuspecting creature."

Ian peered inside the car. Felicia was still grinning and gabbing. Susie slumped in the backseat, nodding and sniffing.

"Dude, chill. Relax. You have to admit, she's unbelievably ho—"

"Of course she's hot, Lance. They're *always* hot. They're often sniffling girls in distress who somehow can't see through your crap, too. God . . ." Ian stalked away from Lance. "We take her home, but that's it. That's *it*. Seriously."

"Fine. Gotcha. Thanks. Good."

Lance threw himself into the Creature and took Susie by the hand.

"It's okay, babe. It's okay. I can't believe some guy would do that to you. I mean . . . not *you*. Come on. It's unthinkable. What a fool." He squeezed her hand and gave her his most sincere, serious look.

"Aawww," said Susie, hanging her head, speaking in a near whisper. "You're the nicest thing, Lance. I can't believe I met someone like you today, of all days."

He wiped a tear from her eye, then squeezed her hand again.

"Shhh," he said, then winked again at Ian.

Ian shook his head. Felicia laughed but made a very strong effort to make the laughter sound like coughing.

"How do we get you home, Susie?" asked Ian.

"Oh, take a left here on highway 252. It's really not too far." Ian turned, pulling onto a rather depressing, empty road. Interstate 65 quickly faded in his rearview mirror.

"So, Lance says you're all from Chicago and you're headed to Charleston," said Susie. "That seems exciting. But you all must be starving. You know, I've got plenty of food back at my place. Just made some cheesy popovers a couple nights ago—I'm famous for 'em. You guys should really stay and eat."

She looked eagerly into Lance's eyes.

"Oh, of course we can," he said. "That's sooo nice of you, Suze. I mean, gosh. Here you are, heartbroken, having this terrible day, and all you can do is think of us, total strangers. You're sweet."

Felicia stared wide-eyed at Ian, who quickly spoke.

"Actually, you know, we're really running very late, Susie. Of course I wish we could—"

"Stay *longer*," said Lance, interrupting. "He wishes we could stay longer. But we've got a long drive ahead. Charleston is . . . well, how far is it, Ian?"

"Ten hours and twenty-one minutes. Roughly."

"So yeah, like Ian says, it's a long drive. We really should go. After eating, of course. That's so nice of you, babe." He paused, looking toward Ian and then back at Susie. "Hey, maybe you could come with us? To Charleston? You could use a little time away, Suze. Some time to clear your head, get away from what's-his-name."

No. No, no, no.

But Ian said nothing. He was frozen by the prospect of confrontation.

"Awww," said Susie. "That is just so nice of you." She leaned against Lance. "I'm so lucky I met you. Feels like I don't meet so many nice folks."

Ian believed her. He stared straight ahead as he drove, seeing only barns, farmhouses, silos, various crops, and the occasional cow. And he just kept driving. Every so often, Susie would say, "Just a li'l farther." So he drove farther. Then she'd say it again. Finally, after slightly more than half an hour of frantic driving, they arrived at a town.

"Well, here we are," said Susie. A tired-looking green sign sagged across the road: BODNER, POP. 151.

The town of Bodner seemed to consist only of a hardware store, a Methodist church, a John Deere dealership, a Lutheran church, a gas station, a Catholic church, a single flashing yellow light suspended above the main (and possibly only) intersection, and a dark storefront with a small sign in the window that read ED'S. It wasn't clear what Ed's was, exactly. Possibly a bar. Or a grocery store. Or a travel agency. Or the headquarters of a vast international crime syndicate—unlikely, but possible. The point was, the sign offered no indication. And Ed was nowhere to be seen. None of Bodner's other 150 citizens were visible either, except for Susie. She lived in a tiny apartment above Ed's. After directing Ian to park along the street, Susie jingled an incredible collection of keys, looking for whichever one would open the door that would lead to the rather dingy carpeted stairwell that would lead, at last, to the front door of her apartment.

Upon entering, Ian found it to be a shockingly bright place. Pink and yellow paint, posters of various male pop stars on the walls, and stacks of fashion magazines on every horizontal surface. When Susie burst in, she immediately flipped the dead bolt, tossed her keys onto a small table—toppling a pile of *Jane*s, *Seventeen*s, and *Cosmo*s—and sank into the cushion of her living room futon. She sighed.

"Gosh, what a day. I still can't believe that fight with Rick." She sniffed, then added, "That jerk."

Lance sat down beside her. "Let it go, Susie." He began to rub her right foot—this was just the sort of too-familiar act that Ian would never have thought to attempt. Susie didn't seem to mind. She looked at Lance rather lovingly.

"Soooo, Susie," began Felicia, idly leafing through a few *People*s, *Glamour*s, and *Star*s. "Didn't you say something earlier about some cheesy Pop-Tarts or something?"

Susie snorted.

"Those'd be my cheesy popovers. I'll warm 'em up!"

She hopped off the futon, allowing Lance to continue the foot rub for a few more seconds before she led him by the hand into the adjacent kitchen.

"Lancey, hon, I need a little help in the kitchen."

Lancey? Did she just call him Lancey?! What the hell is that? That's the second girl in as many days who had called him "Lancey." Good God, I've got to get us out of here. No way Lancey's going to let us leave. But again, Ian said nothing. He merely stared in horror at a picture of a shirtless Ashton Kutcher that had been taped to the wall.

"Lance, could you reach up and get me some aluminum foil?"

Susie gestured toward a flimsy pegboard cabinet door, which Lance slid open. He handed her the roll of foil as she unlatched her refrigerator. The fridge was a relic, like something from a fifties sitcom that got called "the icebox." It emitted a terrible hum. From its depths emerged an uncovered platter of small, flaky pastries.

"My world-famous cheesy popovers!" Susie declared. She hurriedly wrapped them in foil and threw them into her ancient oven, turning a small dial to warm them. As the oven grew hotter, it also began clicking. Loudly.

"I swear," said Susie. "Every appliance around this place makes some crazy noise. But I do love to bake." She popped the plastic lid off a Tupperware container full of sugar cookies. "Just help yourselves."

Ian did. He was starving, after all. So, too, was Felicia, who gobbled cookies alongside him. After a few minutes of quiet eating, Ian looked up and began to address his host.

"Um, Susie, you wouldn't happen to have any milk or any—?"

But Susie had disappeared. Lance, it seemed, had disappeared, too. Felicia spoke.

"They divert our attention with baked goods, then Lance seizes his opportunity. A classic move." She continued eating, not lifting her eyes from a *Seventeen*. "He may be an incorrigible perv, but he does have talent. You can't deny it."

No, Ian couldn't.

Felicia lifted the magazine to her face and read aloud.

"Ian, there's this expert here that says high-school boys think about sex every eleven seconds. That's not possible, right? They must mean, like, every eleven minutes. Or hours. Because you don't think about sex that often, do you, Ian?" She hesitated. "I mean, of course, when you're not online."

"Funny," Ian said, silently wishing that doctors everywhere would just shut the F up about the sex habits of high-school boys. Then he imagined Felicia posing the question in a bikini. *And at a car wash. Or possibly astride a horse. And maybe with Jessica Alba hold–*

"Well, do you, Ian?" Felicia snapped.

"Wha–? Um . . . no. No. Emphatic *no*. I don't think I think about anything that much, really."

Except sex, of course.

"So," he began, "where the heck do you think Lance took our host, Su–?"

"Because if boys did think about sex that much," Felicia said, unable to let the subject go, "that means that just during the course of, say, a fifty-minute trigonometry class–even with saggy old Mr. Kroeger yapping about random formulas–that you, Ian Lafferty, think about sex, oh . . ." She calculated. "About 273 times."

Yup, that sounds about right. Give or take. Depending on what Dana

Beetle is wearing. And whether that headbanger chick Robin What's-her-face shows up. And, of course, if Alexis Higgins—

"Ian, you don't think about sex 273 times during trig, right? Because I'd really have to question how you could possibly still get an A."

"Um, no. No. No, I do not."

"Well, how often do you think about it?"

"During trig?"

"Whenever."

"I don't, um . . . I don't really . . ." He laughed uncomfortably. "I mean, how do I know? I'm not exactly keeping a sex journal, am I?"

"Beats me. You might be. I didn't really think you were the type to drive across the country to visit some cyber-ho, either."

Ouch. Ian considered a variety of potential responses. He really needed an exit strategy for this conversation.

Then came a knock at the door.

Actually, it wasn't so much a knock as a series of powerful thuds, followed by a bellowing voice, followed by more thuds. The voice seemed angry. It was either saying, "Open this damn door, Susie!" or, "I've got a shitload of Uzis!" Ian wasn't entirely sure.

He and Felicia stared at each other.

"Um . . . so should we go see who's at the door?" Ian asked.

"Well, *I* definitely don't go see who's at the door," Felicia answered crisply. "You're the boy. If there's a confrontation that's about to take place, gender roles dictate that you, Ian Lafferty, do the confronting. I'm supposed to cower. And maybe continue eating cookies." She took another bite. The voice continued just outside the door. The room shook with each sequence of knocks.

"Susie should be running in here any second to open the door, yeah? Maybe we should just wait."

More booming knocks. More yelling.

The voice was very clearly saying, "I can hear you, Susie! Now open this frickin' door before I knock it down!"

"Think that might be Rick?" asked Felicia, calmly.

More pounding. The wood of the door sounded as if it was beginning to crack. Still no Susie.

"I really think you should get that, Felicia," said Ian.

"Nuh-uh."

"I don't really think he wants to see some dude when the door opens. I think he'll kill me."

"Maybe he's not that big," Felicia offered.

The door creaked again after another burst of hammering.

"He sounds big. Those are big crunching sounds."

Ian stared at the door as the incessant banging continued. The Kutcher picture fell from the wall. Magazine stacks collapsed. Still no Susie.

She could actually be gone, thought Ian. *There's no way she wouldn't hear this racket. Maybe she's out walking with Lance. "Lancey." Ick. Oh, hell, I should just open the door. Maybe Rick—or whoever—will go away when he sees she's not here.*

"Come on," Ian said to Felicia, grabbing her hand.

"Wha—?"

"We answer the door together. Rick's confusion is our ally."

"Fine," she huffed.

Ian was sweating through his shirt. More pounding at the door.

"Just a sec!" Felicia called to the voice at the door. The pounding ceased.

"Is that you, baby? Sweetie, I'm so sorry. You know how crazy-jealous I get. That's all it was, I swear. Come on, open up. I brought you somethin'."

Ian threw back the deadbolt, and Felicia turned the knob. A grime-covered man with a fistful of daisies pushed open the door. He had a scruffy-looking half-beard and appeared to be in his early twenties.

"Why wouldn't you open the dam—?!"

When he saw Ian and Felicia, he went quiet.

"Hi!" said Ian, in what he quickly realized was exactly the wrong tone.

"Who're you? Where's Susie?"

"We, um . . . that's an excellent question, Rick. You *are* Rick, right?" Ian asked.

The man in the doorway patted the name patch on his stained denim work shirt. It read, RICK W., SERVICE TECHNICIAN.

"Right," said Ian. "Well, Rick, we've heard a lot about you. From Susie."

"And where the hell is she?"

"Um, right. Not here. We think. No, not here. But we are." Ian paused. "We're here. But not Susie. Not anymore."

Rick tensed, then moved to within inches of Ian.

"Who are you?" he said tersely.

"Ian. Ian Lafferty." Ian extended his hand, which Rick did not take. "And this is Felicia. We're—"

"Susie's cousins," said Felicia. "We're not from around here, Rick. But Susie called me today so I drove down. She was upset—really upset. Something about her jackass boyfriend." With that, Felicia struck a rather assertive pose, with her hands at her hips and a smirk on her face.

Oh God. Very bad move. Very bad. Ian braced himself for Rick's forthcoming attack.

But Rick seemed to soften. He stepped back.

"I, well . . . okay. I know I was a little bit of a jackass." Rick wouldn't look Felicia in the eye. "But I am real sorry." He shifted his weight, staring at his beaten leather work boots. "I just gotta see Susie. Where is she?"

"We're not sure," said Felicia, still speaking sternly. "She gave us a plate of cookies and then just sneaked off. She's in a really fragile state right now, Dick."

"Rick."

"Whatever, Dick. Wherever Susie is, you can believe she doesn't want to talk to you. I really think you should leave."

Rick was silent for a protracted moment. Then his head perked up. He sniffed the air.

"Are those Susie's popovers?"

"The world-famous ones," said Ian.

"I can't believe she'd just leave with her popovers in the oven." He looked at Ian. "Are you sure she's not here?"

"Do you see her, *Dick*?" Felicia asked. "You really need to leave." She stared at Rick while Rick, in turn, glared at Ian. *"Leave,"* she repeated. An uncomfortable moment passed in silence before Rick began to backpedal.

Then, somewhere at the rear of the apartment, a lamp fell with a crash.

Then a distinctly male voice said, "Oh, shit!"

Then—after taking a fraction of a second to process these happenings—

Rick tossed Ian onto the futon. He sprinted down a hallway that led, presumably, to the fallen lamp and the oh-shitter. Felicia followed him toward a closed door at the end of the hall. Rick threw it open, then stopped cold. Felicia froze behind him.

Easing himself off the futon mattress, Ian hurried down the hall toward the doorway, too. Before he, too, could see what Rick and Felicia were gawking at, he heard Lance's voice.

"Oh, hi. Hey there, Felicia. Who's, um . . . who's your friend? Can he fix lamps? Heh."

Upon reaching Felicia, Ian looked into what was clearly Susie's bedroom. Amid the expected clutter of magazines, makeup, and plush animals, he also saw a pile of clothing–most of it Lance's. Lance himself stood in a far corner of the room. He appeared to be completely naked, except for a small Hello Kitty blanket wrapped about his waist. The pieces of the fallen lamp were at his feet. Susie stood at the opposite end of the room. She was adjusting her top– possibly reattaching a bra, Ian thought–and smoothing her very small skirt.

"Rick!" she said, offering a weak attempt at surprised expression. Rick dropped the daisies.

"Who's *that* guy? Another cousin?" He stalked slowly toward Lance.

"Another what?" Susie asked, confused.

"I can't believe you, Susie! How could you?" Rick looked toward Lance menacingly. "You're mine, assho–"

"I'm sorry, Rick!" said Susie. "But you broke up with me! Big jerkball. I cried all day . . . all day." Felicia hid a laugh. Ian cringed.

Susie continued. "Anyway, we didn't *do* it. I was just . . . I dunno. . . . You really hurt me, Rick."

"I didn't mean to totally break up, Susie. I mean, I love you. But *you* . . ." His eyes were locked on Lance. " . . . I don't know and I certainly don't love." Rick's chest and shoulders pressed forward, as if he were an animal in some territorial battle attempting to look as threatening as possible. He walked forward, cracking his knuckles. "And here you are, preying on my sad, brokenhearted girlfriend. I think someone needs to teach you a lesson—"

"A lesson? What kind of lesson?" Lance let out a little squeak.

Felicia leaned back and whispered in Ian's ear.

"Let me handle this. You grab the popovers."

With that, she launched herself past an angry Rick, sliding under the frilly canopy of Susie's four-poster bed, and delivered a punch directly to Lance's midsection. He fell against the wall and slumped to the floor, nearly dropping the blanket. He groaned.

"What the hell, Feli—?"

"Rick is right! Someone *does* need to teach you a lesson! Me, your girlfriend! What the *hell*, Lance?! We're not here ten minutes and my boyfriend is scamming on my *allegedly* brokenhearted cousin?!" Felicia glared at Susie, then slugged Lance in the shoulder. Then she slugged him again. And again.

Lance stared at Felicia, half perplexed and half terrified.

"Whoa," said Rick, backing up. "That girl sure can hit."

"You're, like, boyfriend/girlfriend?" asked Susie. "F'real? I swear I didn't know, Felicia. Lance, how could you?!"

Lance rubbed his shoulder.

"Yeah!" exclaimed Felicia. "How could you, Lance?!" She slapped him.

Rick let out a little laugh. "It looks like your woman is going to handle this."

Felicia grabbed Lance by the arm, wrenched him to his feet, and kicked his shin. She nodded at Rick. "You bet I am." Lance hopped forward on his other leg, still managing to clutch the Hello Kitty blanket.

"Out!" she yelled. "Get outta here, Lance. Now! We're going! Grab your damn clothes, asshat!"

Felicia stomped ahead violently. Lance gathered his pile of clothes and followed her quietly.

As Felicia approached Ian in the hallway, she whispered again, "Seriously, Ian, get the popovers. They smell delicious." Then she called out to Susie, "We're so gone. Glad my boyfriend could comfort you in your time of need, trollop."

"But I *swear* I didn't know, Felicia!" called Susie. She and Rick stood together, confused, in Susie's bedroom.

Ian scrambled ahead, located an oven mitt, and grabbed the popovers. He calmly trailed a fake-angry Felicia and a legitimately naked Lance as they exited the apartment.

When they hit the stairwell that led to the street, they began to run.

Lance shot out of the small building, past the Ed's sign, and slid over the trunk of Ian's car, dropping a sock on the curb. Ian bent down to retrieve it.

"Leave the damn sock!" shouted a panicky Lance. "Drive, Ian! Drive! That Rick dude could be following us! And I bet he drives some bitchin'-fast El Camino! Or, like, a pickup with a gun in the back! And some kind of killer pit bull!" Ian abandoned the sock and hurried around to the front of the Creature.

"C'mon!" urged Lance.

"Relax, spaz-monkey." Ian tried to give him a firm look, but it soon morphed into a laugh. Lance stood in the street, barefoot and discombobulated, with Hello Kitty's giant face over his pelvis. Felicia snickered. All three were breathing heavily from the short sprint, but only Lance seemed truly frightened.

"I should so leave you here, Lance. Alone. Naked. Scared, like a ninny." Ian opened the doors. Lance plunged into the backseat.

"Please drive," he said.

Ian spun the Creature around, kicking up dirt from the desolate main street of Bodner, Indiana. Lance peered up through the Creature's rear window toward Susie's apartment.

"I don't see anything," he said, still panting from the race to the car. "How fast can the Creature move, dude? Let's test it. Open it up. Rev the engine and such."

"Well, it can't move fast enough to make up the time we lost while you tried to get it on with Susie." Ian paused. "I mean, jeez. No more side trips, Lance. None. Zero."

Ian made a sharp turn, heading back to the interstate. The Creature fishtailed for an instant, then caught the pavement and accelerated toward the low sun.

"Come on," said Lance. "You have to admit she was a cutie, eh?"

"Lance, you can have all the sex you want with whatever you want when we get back home. But I swear, if you waste another second of this trip—for any reason at all—you're getting left behind." Ian paused. "And please put some clothes on."

Lance threw his clothes onto the rear seat next to him, taking a quick inventory to make certain that he'd only lost a single sock. Then he held up his boxers.

"Ian, I've got another quick lesson for you. Just so you can salvage something from this admittedly disappointing portion of the drive." He extended the plaid cotton boxers toward the front seat. "Do you notice anything unusual about these?"

"Gross, Lance," said Felicia. "Those need to get on you. Quickly."

"No peeking back here, Felicia."

"Oh, don't worry," she said. "I've seen all of you I care to see."

"So, Ian," said Lance. "Do you notice anything unusual?"

"Can this be a rhetorical question?" Ian said. "Because I really don't want to look at your underthings."

"Sure, fine. Rhetorical. Well, the point is, there is *nothing* unusual about my boxers. Nothing. That is, they won't cause a girl to gasp or panic or run out of bed, screaming for her mother. They're not an impediment."

"And what's your point?" Ian asked. "You think I've got some funky leather-and-zipper thing for Danielle? Because I don't. So don't worry."

"No, it's just . . . you have a reputation."

"Huh?"

"Wha—?" said Felicia.

"Remember the Greg Blanc sleepover of '98, Ian?"

"Lance, I was, like, eleven."

"You had yellow underwear, Ian."

"It was not *yellow* underwear, Lance. It was *Chewbacca* underwear. Which is totally different."

"They were yellow, Ian."

"They were Underoos." Ian's speedometer climbed past ninety. "They were very cool. And anyway, it's not like I still have 'em. I'm sure they don't fit."

"Well, what I'm saying is this: nothing geeky under the clothes, Ian. No *Battlestar Galactica* undershirts, no Boba Fett medallions, no Power Rangers briefs, no—"

"I get it. And I appreciate your concern, Lance. Now please put the boxers on."

"Tell me about these Power Rangers undies, Ian," said Felicia. "That's hot. Seriously."

"Oh, shut up."

"Hmm. I don't think I will." She wheeled around to address Lance. "Hey, how 'bout some props for me? That guy would've mauled you if I hadn't pretended to be your girlfriend—the idea of which disgusts me, by the way. Rick was pretty pissed. And large."

"You kick *hard*, dude. Unnecessarily hard. My shin is killing me. I should have you arrested for assault." He paused. "But thanks. I would've been fighting Rick with a handicap, what with the lack of clothing."

"Um . . . not to mention your lack of fighting. Ever. In your life. Pretty boy." She sniffed her pilfered batch of popovers. "Mmmm, cheese."

Hurry, Ian told himself. He was growing irritated. *The schedule is totally shot. No more stopping. Might have to renegotiate the pee breaks, too. We could be in Kentucky by now if it weren't for pee breaks. And if it weren't for Lance.*

He spun a knob on the car stereo, looking for any station that happened to be playing something that suited his mood—which, at the time, would have only been some sort of caustic death metal. He found nothing but country music, farm reports, and the occasional Indianapolis top forty station. Frustrated, he flipped off the radio.

"Hope Susie's all right with that Rick guy," said Lance. "Do you think we should go ba—?"

"Don't say it, Lance. I'm sure she's fine," said Ian. "They're probably having a nice, rational, adult discussion about relationships right now. She's fine."

"They're probably doing some heavy makeup lovin' right now," said Felicia, smirking. "Popover?" She extended the lukewarm pastries toward Ian first, then Lance.

"No, thanks," said Ian.

"Later," said Lance. "Maybe after dinner. We're stopping soon, right? Where should we eat?"

"You're eating in the backseat, Lance," said Ian, plainly miffed. "Plenty of chips in the bag. Felicia has her popovers. I have my fruit pies. We drive."

"That is sooo not right. It's just deeply not right. Maybe just a quick value meal? Steak n Shake? Arby's? Taco Be—?"

"No. Do you know what's not right, Lance? We've driven, like, six miles and you're still naked."

"The boy has a Hello Kitty fetish," Felicia said.

"You'd be surprised by my fetishes."

"Oh, I really doubt that."

Lance began to dress himself. Felicia flipped the radio back on, found an Indianapolis station playing seventies and eighties hits, and began singing along in an absurdly loud and entirely atonal voice. When he was partial to a song and not busy devouring Doritos, Lance joined her.

Ian, however, did not sing. Nor did he speak. He simply sped through the rural countryside, past the same cows, crops, silos, and barns he'd passed en route to Bodner. He mentally replayed all the missteps and screwups that had resulted in such an unwise and unnecessary detour. By the time he reached I-65, he'd thought himself into a very pissed-off, anxious state.

Felicia addressed him between songs.

"Ian, maybe we could just pull off for a minute and—"

"No."

"Aren't you even a little bit—?"

"No."

"But we wouldn't have to—"

"No."

"It's just that we don't have any real food in this—"

"Nuh-uh."

Ian's eyes were fixed on the road. Felicia giggled.

"You know, Ian, you'll have to perk up a little for Danielle. This sullen mood will never do."

"And," Lance added, spraying a bit of orange Dorito dust into the air, "moods like yours can contribute to erectile dysfun—hey, is this Dexys Midnight Runners?! Sweet!" Lance jabbed a finger toward the radio. "Hey, this is some classic crap! Crank that up!"

Ian did nothing. Felicia twisted the volume knob on the Creature's aged radio. She and Lance grooved in their seats, shouting lyrics above the rush of air through the windows.

> *"At this moment, you mean everything*
> *With you in that dress*
> *My thoughts, I confess*
> *Verge on dirty. . . ."*

Ian wove through traffic, using all lanes to pass all cars. He wished he could feel relaxed enough to sing. Felicia and Lance's bruising duets lasted until something like 8 P.M. Their whining about the lack of food and drink lasted considerably longer.

Lance: "C'mon. You're killing us. I'm so thirsty."

Ian: "Drink your spit."

Felicia: "Yuk. But I am that desperate."

And so it went. Felicia began to devour the popovers quietly, occasionally making a satisfied sound. The Creature rolled through the hot countryside, south into Kentucky. Finally drained of all enthusiasm, Lance and Felicia positioned themselves for sleep after a rare gas/beverage/pee stop. Lance sprawled across the rear of the Creature, his head resting on the foam doughnut costume, which Ian had generously retrieved from the trunk. Felicia tilted back the passenger seat, tucking her feet in the nook between the dashboard and windshield.

"Ian," mumbled Felicia at 11:02. "You never finished telling me—" She yawned. "How often you think about sex."

"Infrequently enough to still ace trig. But frequently enough to be here, driving through the South at ninety miles an hour."

"Weird," said Felicia, sighing. A moment passed. She yawned again. "Aren't you tired, Ian?"

"No, I'm good."

"Because we could stop. I feel a little queasy."

"You just need sleep. I'm fine. I'll drive."

"How far?"

"Dunno. Straight through the night. Or until I pass out and we plunge off a cliff and die a fiery death. 'Too fast to live,' they'll say. 'Too young to—'"

"'To get laid.'"

Ian laughed self-consciously. Felicia continued her yawning.

"I have things to say to you, Ian. But it's never—"

Lance threw his lone sock into the front.

"Shut up, already," he muttered. "There are sleepy people back here."

"It's never the right time, exactly." Felicia lowered her window and flung the sock somewhere into the thick weeds along the interstate.

"That's not nice," said Lance, unmoving. He and Felicia were soon asleep. A determined Ian Lafferty kept driving.

He did, in fact, drive straight through the night.

After speeding through the moonless evening along various highways, Ian stopped and watched the Saturday sun rise at a highway rest stop somewhere, he was pretty sure, in North Carolina. He had intended to find a pop machine and replenish his supply of severely caffeinated beverages. But after he'd thrown the car into park, Ian had suddenly had a difficult time moving. He was way past exhausted, bordering on delirious. He began reciting, for no specific reason, various doughnut combinations that equaled one dozen.

"Three Bavarian kremes, three powdered sugar, three lemon bursts, two jelly filled, one cinnamon cake." He stretched, accidentally poking Felicia's left arm. She stirred but didn't wake. "Two apple 'n' spice, two apple crumb cake, five glazed, three double chocolate." The clock read 6:47. "All righty. Six chocolate frosted—wait, no, make that six chocolate coconuts, two Boston kremes—an excellent choice—

two marble frosted, and two vanilla kremes." He yawned. "Three strawberry frosted, two chocolate Bismarcks . . ."

Lance sat upright, poked his head into the front, and spoke in a half-whisper.

"What're you doing, dude?"

"Nothing. Nothing, nothing, nothing. A little memory exercise. With doughnuts." Ian spoke slowly, like a ten-year-old reading a difficult sentence aloud in class. "Yup. Doughnuts, doughnuts, doughnuts."

Lance laughed. "It's like you're high. And jonesin' for a bakery."

"Nope, nope, nope. Not high. Just a little tired. But nothing, um . . ."

Ian ceased talking. He stared glassy-eyed at the rest stop's snack area.

"Nothing *what*, dude?"

"Nothing what? Oh. Nothing. I was just saying I was tired. But nothing that a little caffeine couldn't take care of. And high-fructose corn syrup." Ian turned to face Lance. *"Fructose."* He smiled. "Mmmmm."

"Ian, I don't think you should drive anymore. You need some sleep—serious sleep. You're cooked." Lance reached behind Ian to unlock his door. "Hop out of the car, buddy. Just climb in back and lie down. I'll do some driving."

"Hop? Hop, hop, hop. I am tired, that's true." With that, Ian flipped himself backward over the driver's seat, clipping Felicia's nose with his shoe and landing elbow-first in Lance's lap.

"Um . . . ick. Please get off me."

Felicia squirmed, then lifted her head. She squinted at Ian and Lance, cupping a hand to her nose.

"What's up? God, I feel terrible. Where are we?"

"We have traversed Kentucky," said Ian happily. "The Bluegrass State. Home of, um . . . horses. And presumably bluegrass. But it was dark–I couldn't really tell. Anyway, traversed it we have. And we've traversed Tennessee, home of . . well, I don't know. Home to nothing much that I could actually see. But I've heard they make nice music or something. Now I think we're in North Carolina, home of . . . um, it was once home to Michael Jordan. But not anymore." Ian paused. "Hey, there are some pop machines over there. I'm very tired, Felicia."

Lance climbed over the seat somewhat more capably than Ian had, easing himself behind the steering wheel and striking no one in the process.

"Okay, I'll drive. I've never driven the Creature. But I've seen it done. She's a big mother. But what the hell, right?"

"That's the spirit," offered Ian. "Be careful with her, please. I love her so. The map is right up front. Between the seats. Lance, do not deviate from the predetermined route. Felicia, do not let Lance deviate from the route. I'm going to attempt to sleep in a semi-aware state. Like a whale. So, if Lance *does* deviate from the route–or attempts to pick up another gas station employee–I will know."

"Like a whale? What does that *mean*?" asked Lance.

"Semi-conscious. When a whale sleeps, only half its brain is actually resting. The whale keeps moving. So it can surface. To breathe. With its blowhole." Ian yawned. "Dolphins, too. And that'll be me. Semiconscious." He yawned again.

"Dude, keep your blowhole in the backseat. Go to sleep. With your whole brain."

"Whatever. The point is this: do not deviate from the predetermined route. Felicia, help him."

She rubbed her eyes. "Ugh. I really feel crappy. I think maybe I need breakfast." Felicia slid out of the car and ambled toward the snack area.

"I need a pop, too," said Lance, opening his door. "Sleep, Ian."

"Right." Ian closed his eyes and began to recline. Then a thought struck him. "Oh, Lance. Hand me that Toady. It's on top of the map— the one with the route from which . . . "

" . . . I cannot deviate. Right. Got it." Lance handed Ian the device. "No deviation. Try to keep the steamy chat to a minimum back there, tiger. Get to sleep. You have to be fit to perform today."

This brought a shudder of panic to Ian. He wanted to e-mail Danielle but needed to fall into fake-Ian mode to do so. And fake-Ian didn't worry about being fit to perform. *Just say something short, something flippant*, he told himself. *Let her know you're on the way. But don't be desperate. Don't even be happy. Commit in a way that's noncommittal. Nothing too nice. What would Lance say?*

He began to stab at the keys.

To: dmorrison@scsu.edu

From: ilafferty@toady.com

Subject: Dispatch from the road

Hella good trip so far, MT. But I strayed from the map. Should be there sometime tonight-ish.

Wear something slinky. Or see-through. Or maybe
nothing.

Ian

That'll do. He stared at the device in his hand. *That was creepy, too.*
Ian clutched the Toady to his chest like a stuffed bear. Within a
minute, with the sunlight creeping overhead and birds chirping in the
trees, he fell asleep.

It was a fitful sleep. Ian's face pressed into the hot foam of the doughnut costume, causing him to wake periodically in small puddles of
drool, chocolate, and sweat. He was not, however, able to use these
brief periods of whalelike half-consciousness to assess Lance's
progress on the road. Instead, at these moments he would simply roll
his face over to a dry patch of doughnut and drift off again. But if he
had been able to assess Lance's roadway progress, he would not have
been pleased.

Ian awoke to the sound of nearby laughter—unrestrained laughter.
It sounded like Felicia and Lance. The car was not moving. The sun
was baking everything inside. Ian thought he heard the same birds
chirping in the same trees. But that couldn't be possible. Because that
would mean . . .

They hadn't moved.

Ian shot upright and blinked his eyes. The Creature was still in the same parking spot at the same rest stop. Felicia and Lance were sitting atop the hood, laughing. More accurately, Felicia was rolling on the hood, shaking with spasms of laughter as Lance read something aloud. It was apparently something so uproariously funny that the impending loss of Ian Lafferty's virginity would have to wait.

How long have I been sleeping?

Ian's pulse leaped. He was fully awake.

He reached into the front seat and honked the Creature's horn. A startled Felicia rolled off the hood, sending up a small plume of dirt when she hit the ground. Lance jumped off the front of the Creature and spun around. In his right hand he held Ian's Toady.

Oh. Crap.

Felicia's head popped up on the passenger side of the car. Smirking, she patted the dirt from her clothes and approached. "Ian, if the stuff we've been reading weren't so damned funny, I'd really be pissed at you. I mean, I'm still pissed at you—'Tasty.' But I'd *really* be pissed if it all weren't so funny." She shook her head. "Very sad, yet very funny."

Crap.

Ian's anger at waking up still at the rest stop had been largely eclipsed. He was, at that moment, swimming in humiliation. He did not respond to Felicia. She and Lance had almost certainly been reading his correspondence with Danielle, a collection of e-mails rife with fallacies, absurdities, and things far worse.

He spied the key in the ignition. He turned it just far enough to power the Creature's clock. It was 10:39. He had meant to be in Charleston long before 10:39 on Saturday.

But instead, he was preparing to be mocked. Crestfallen, he exited the Creature.

Lance bolted toward him, his left hand raised to solicit a high five. "Ian, this is awesome. *Awesome.* Funny, and a little out there—even by my standards—but awesome." He waved his upraised hand. "C'mon, give it up!"

Ian offered a meek, hesitant high five.

"Dude, I am stoked!" exclaimed Lance, whacking Ian's hand. "Here I thought you had talked some desperate, egg-shaped chess-club chick into letting you grope her in her dorm room. But no, Ian. No, you *went* for it. This girl has serious potential."

Ian felt both flattered and embarrassed. Mostly embarrassed. Felicia contorted her face, staring at Lance.

"Of course you'd congratulate him, perv. Evil psycho perv. Let me get this straight: Ian lies to this Danielle person—who, by the way, is an idiot for even being remotely interested in the guy Ian's pretending to be—then he *lies to us* about lying to the girl." She paused, looking toward Ian, then back at Lance. "And you're giving Ian high fives for basically lying his ass off. To everyone."

She turned her back, as if for dramatic effect, then spun around again. "And do I need to mention that he lied to his parents? Well, he did." She then broke into a halfway-decent impression of Ian. "'Oh, Mom and Dad, I'm with Lance and Felicia downtown. . . . Oh, Lance and Felicia, I'm at my grandmother's deathbed. . . . Oh, Internet ho, I'm on my way. And I'm this incredibly cool guy. Too cool for you, Miss Tasty. (Did you catch that? Called you 'Miss Tasty.' Because I'm that cool.) But anyway, if you'll have sex with me, I guess we could hang out and stuff.'" She glared at Ian.

"What happened to 'If it weren't so funny, I'd be pissed'?" he said sheepishly. "And I do not sound that nasally." Ian looked at Lance. "I don't, right?"

Lance shrugged, nodding.

"Well," began Felicia, "I guess the more I think about how you've been trying to play everyone—which isn't like you at all. Or at least it never used to be like you—well, yeah. Now I'm less amused. I'm pretty much just pissed."

"You have to admit," offered Lance, "his approach worked. Asshole-ifying himself. It totally worked. This chick digs him. That's the key with hotties. You've got to let them know you're not intimidated by their hotness. A few insults, a few crass remarks—that's all it takes. And now this chick—this fantastically burnin'-hot chick— is all into you, Ian."

"This *chick*," Felicia said indignantly, "doesn't know the first thing about Ian Lafferty. Does she know that he can act out *Rocky III* with sock puppets? No. Does she know that he slept with a stuffed stego-saurus until he was, like, thirteen, and that the same stegosaurus is, to this day, conspicuously close to his bed? No. Does she know that he was always the last person picked for sports in gym—and not be-cause he couldn't play, but because he was too freakin' analytical and it aggravated his teammates? No. She doesn't know *shit* about Ian!"

Felicia took a breath, then said, "God, I think I'm gonna hurl."

"Okay," said Lance. "So maybe a few of the things he told this Danielle chick were ill-advised. But I'm still proud of Ian. It's not like he can go braggin' on his stegosaurus and expect women to fel-late him."

"Um . . . yuk," said Felicia.

"Oh, please." Lance turned to Ian. "It's like I've been telling you: the nice-guy thing rarely works. Okay, with that what's-her-name girl back in Podunk, Indiana, it was working—"

"Susie? In Bodner?" said Felicia. "Hello. It was yesterday. And her boyfriend nearly killed you."

"—but it only worked because of extenuating circumstances. If she hadn't been breaking up with that crazy hayseed dude, *nice* wouldn't have gotten me a smile. Normally if you're cultivating a relationship with a hottie, the last thing you wanna be is nice. And the second-to-last thing you wanna be is yourself—whoever you are. Whether you're me, Orlando Bloom, Flava Flav—I don't care. Whoever you are, you've gotta be just a little bit assholier."

"That's twisted," said Felicia. "You tell him things like this often, Lance? You have no real feelings toward women whatsoever, do you? You just think of us as penis receptacles, is that right? Women are just places to put Li'l Lance?"

"Okay, the 'Li'l' stuff is unnecessary. And derogatory. And no, I'm not *just* looking for places to put my penis. If I were, I'd get one of those life-size inflatable dolls."

"You might find a rubber doll too intellectually challenging, Lance. They're a notch above one of your typical girls," said Felicia.

"So I don't administer IQ tests before I hit on girls. Whatever. I'm not some elitist snob. And it's not like I mess around with them just to boost my self-esteem." He paused. "I'm basically like anybody else, I think." He looked at his feet, then spoke a little softer. "Look, I'd like to meet the right girl. I'd like to be in a relationship. I'd like to find someone I really mesh with, where everything . . . I dunno . . . just *fits*."

He paused again. "And I'm not talking about my penis fitting, Felicia. Just so we're clear."

She snickered almost involuntarily. "What about all these girls you leave by the wayside—after doing whatever with them—when it turns out you don't think you've 'meshed'? Do you even care?"

"Well, yeah. Sure I care. Anyway, I like to think I've maybe left them with some pleasant memories."

Felicia glared at Lance unsympathetically. "So twisted," she finally said.

"But, um, anyway . . . can we talk about Ian again?" stammered Lance. "It still sucks you lied to us."

"Exactly," said Felicia.

"I know." Ian sighed. "You're totally right. And I'm sorry for not being straight with you. For not telling the truth. That is, I'm sorry that I didn't tell you the truth *yesterday* at Walgreens when I was apologizing for not telling you the full truth before. For which I'm also very sorry." He sighed. "This isn't me. It's really not."

"But it's working," said Lance.

"I dunno, Felicia. I was just screwing around. I didn't think things would get this far with Danielle. Honestly. It's just that, well, the cruder I was, the more she seemed to like me. And I'm not really accustomed to receiving attention from hot girls. Unless they're ordering doughnuts. Which, it turns out, hot girls don't do so often."

"Oh, please," said Lance. "You say what you have to say to a girl to get where you want to go. You have to differentiate yourself from the pack. I once told a chick I was an exchange student from Ghana. Spoke with an accent and everything."

"Did that work?"

"No. She called bullshit on me. Turns out they don't have Australian accents in Ghana. Who knew? But the thing is, you try what you have to try—and you say what you have to say—to get the girl. So I like where your head is on this, Ian."

"That's so despicable, Lance," said Felicia.

"Dude, if I vetted all my pickup attempts with you, I'd only hook up with brainy punk-rock freaks and girls who are pretty *on the inside*. Which isn't the only place that I want them to be pretty." Lance slugged Ian's shoulder lightly. "I'm glad to see that my advice has sunk in. I'm touched. I like the way you selectively blow her off, but you give her just enough fake Ian to make her come back. You're good. But you're also really out there with this girl. There's some crazy stuff in here."

Lance waved the Toady.

"Such as?" asked Ian.

"Well, like all this Northwestern crap."

"That's not crazy. I've got the grades. I've got the test scores. I'm no dummy."

"You're also no football player."

"Oh," said Ian. "That."

Lance toggled through e-mails and text messages, then began to read.

"'Gotta go, Tasty. Football practice at three.'" He toggled again. "'Can't talk. Off for beers with the O-line.'" More toggling. "'Practice sucked. Very sore. But pain is for puss—'"

Ian snatched the Toady from Lance's hand.

"Okay, enough!" he said.

"What position do you play, tiger?" asked Lance, smirking.

"I could be a *kicker*," Ian said, glancing at his thin arms. "But I'll concede that, in hindsight, it seems a little dumb. Maybe very dumb. But I never expected to actually *meet* this girl. It was just an act. Almost an experiment."

"Well," Felicia said, "the experiment landed us all here. In the middle of, um . . . where? Tennessee is it? Or did we make it to North Carolina? Wherever it is, it's about a thousand degrees. Man, do I feel like crap." She scrunched up her face. "I hope you do too, Ian."

"I do. But, you know, um . . . I *tried* to leave you guys out of this." He looked at Lance. "Speaking of North Carolina, why are we still here? I was out for, like, just a few hours. You were going to drive. We should be in South Carolina. I should be with Danielle doing who knows what."

"It wasn't my fault, dude," Lance said. "I swear. No cuties to be found at this rest stop. Only fat, surly truckers. But Felicia didn't feel well." Lance's voice fell to a whisper. "A slight digestive malady—the big D, Ian. Many runs to the bathroom. Not pretty. She wasn't roadworthy." Lance resumed speaking at normal volume. "So we decided to chill, maybe get a snack, let her stomach settle. And then, well . . . your Toady was just sitting there."

"On top of me."

"Right. I mean, it could've easily fallen. Or something. So I picked it up." He paused. "And I was bored. And curious. And, you know . . . Felicia was just sort of moaning. So I started to read."

"But how'd you get my password?"

"It didn't exactly require a master computer hacker, Ian. It was, like, the third *Star Wars* character I guessed."

"Oh."

Ian fell silent. He checked the Toady for new messages, but found none. He sent a quick text:

Went 2 sleep. WOOps. B there soon, Tasty. L8r . . .

What if Danielle's given up on me? She probably should. What if she's as freaked about this visit as I am? What if—oh, hell. I've come this far.

"Let's get going," he said. "I'm driving. Felicia, if you still feel icky, let's get you something carbonated to dri—"

As if on cue, Felicia lurched forward, steadied herself against the Creature's fender, and began to puke.

Once she began puking, it was *on*. Felicia was like a zook factory, belching forth jets of foul-smelling, Technicolor, partially digested foodstuff. Lance and Ian recoiled.

"Don't just stand there," she gasped, then heaved again. "Help me." She groaned. "Get me some—"

More zooking.

"Get me some kinda towel or mayb—"

More zooking.

"Maybe a bucke—"

Still more zooking.

"Gross," Lance finally said. "You shouldn't have had those Skittles for breakfast. They were probably, like, a hundred years old."

Ian tucked his Toady under the driver's seat of the Creature, then ran to Felicia. He held her left hand and wrapped an arm around her shoulder.

"Oh God, Ia—"

Further zooking. Ian hopped to the side, narrowly eluding a colorful stream. Regurgitated Skittles clacked against the asphalt of the parking lot.

"I think it's the popov—"

Zook.

"It's the popovers. I'm the only one who ate the popo—"

Zook.

"Okay, stop talking," said Ian, pulling a few loose strands of hair away from her clammy face. "You're gonna be all right. Let's sit." He opened the passenger-side door and eased Felicia down. She jerked forward and puked again and, as if playing hopscotch, Ian quickly spread his feet to avoid a direct hit.

"Sorry," she mouthed.

"No worries," Ian replied. "Lance, get me something to clean this poor girl up with, please."

Lance arrived with the foam doughnut suit and began to wipe at the edges of her mouth. Before the dangers of this move could fully register with Ian, Felicia had projectile-vomited directly into the costume's neck hole, coating the interior.

"No!" Ian yelped, far too late.

"Sorry 'bout tha—"

Zook.

"Oh, Felicia, it's not your fault. It's not your fault at all."

"Sorry," said Lance.

"It *is* very much your fault, Lance. My boss is gonna *kill* me. And then he's gonna fire me. Then he'll kill me some more. He loves this suit."

"Maybe he'll just make you rock the doughnut on Monday. Before it's cleaned."

Felicia heaved.

"Oh, Ian," she moaned.

"It's gotta be the popovers. Those things had a nasty look about them. Why do you think Ian and I steered clear?"

"Well, that woulda been a very helpful observation for you to make yester—"

Heave.

"Yesterday. But today, your comments are most unwelc—"

Another heave.

"*Most* unwelcome. Oh, God . . ." She slumped against Ian's leg.

Pools of cheesy puke splatter covered the ground near the Creature. The heat was oppressive. Ian gripped Felicia's hands. He told her to breathe.

"Dude, we should get her to a hospital," said Lance.

"Oh, come on, I'm just—" She burped. "Oh, no." She rose to her feet and staggered off behind the car to vomit in semi-privacy.

"Seriously," Lance said to Ian. "She should see a doctor. My dad's old golf pro Bernard got food poisoning from shrimp scampi. He lost twenty pounds. Suddenly he's slicing the ball, he can't hit a fairway, he's short off the tee. Pretty soon he's an ex–golf pro. And my mom said her cousin knew someone when they were kids who ate an undercooked pork chop and caught some kind of weird parasite and *died*."

"That's terrible."

Felicia coughed loudly, then began sobbing. Ian rushed to her side, splashing through cheese puddles. She grew weak-kneed and slouched against him.

"I feel awful. It's like *Alien*. Like some toothy space larva is chewing its way through me. God, Ian. This really su—"

More retching.

"Lance is right. We should get you to a doctor."

"You and I have to talk, Ian. We need to talk abou—"

Another heave.

"Seriously. You need a doctor."

She looked up at him with red, teary eyes.

"Mmm-kay."

Ian wrapped the doughnut costume in a plastic Walgreens bag, threw it back into the trunk, then started the car. The Creature whipped out of the rest stop and headed south. Ian had no idea where to find a hospital, nor did he know what the ramifications of an emergency room visit might be. *Will they have to call her parents? And won't her parents be just incredibly pissed off? Will that bring this trip to an immediate halt?* Ian didn't care. He was overwhelmed with worry. He'd never seen anyone suddenly become so violently ill. Felicia moaned in the Creature's backseat, her head tilted toward an open window. Occasionally she leaned out and disgorged a few more mushy particles from her digestive system along the interstate (and along the side of Ian's car. Again, not that he cared). Ian felt confident that a few hours earlier, just before he'd pulled into the rest stop, he'd seen a road sign directing travelers to gas, food, and hotel options at some nearby exit. He raced along, hoping that such amenities also meant that this backwoodsy area could support a hospital.

After traveling no more than a mile, he indeed noticed a road sign that read, GAS, LODGING, FOOD, NEXT EXIT. Underneath these words was the insignia of an establishment—probably a restaurant, Ian decided—called Woody's.

"We'll get off here and ask directions to the nearest hospital. Just hang on, Felicia."

She nodded, then burped, then groaned, then emitted a small, weak cry.

"Please, Ian," she said. "Call me 'Miss Tasty.' I love it when you call me sexy names." She stuck her head out the window again, awaiting the next ripple of discomfort.

"Nice to see you're still able to make fun of me. That way I know you're still clinging to life."

Ian hardly slowed down as he steered onto the exit ramp toward something called Highway 114. Another Woody's sign awaited. Underneath the insignia was an arrow pointing right, and the words, TWO MILES, GOOD EATS. The highway ahead appeared entirely empty. Ian accelerated the Creature. The speedometer inched past a hundred miles and hour, and the car's engine squealed in resistance.

"Woo-hoo. You go, Ian," said Lance.

Felicia moaned. "Is there some latent, male fast-drivey thing happening here? Because it's not making me feel any better."

"Sorry, Felicia." He eased back to ninety, and the Creature's disposition seemed to improve.

They whizzed past another Woody's sign. GAS, DIESEL, it read. Then they passed another Woody's sign. It read, VACANCY. COLOR TV, CABLE, HBO.

"Must be some place, this Woody's," said Ian.

"That'd probably be it," said Lance, pointing toward a complex of smallish structures about a quarter mile away. Each building appeared to be made of plywood and corrugated metal. A forty-foot-tall inflatable gorilla sat at the entrance to the complex's driveway. A giant hand-painted sign soon came into view:

WELCOME TO WOODY'S!

GAS, LIQUOR, MOTEL, MINI-GOLF, DELI, AMMO, ADULT BOOKS

"No doubt Woody must have some kind of advanced medical center here, too," said Lance.

Felicia grunted.

Ian veered onto the dirt driveway, past the windowless adult bookstore and the frayed gray-green turf of the mini-golf course. He parked the Creature near a rather old-fashioned gas pump. A disheveled attendant in blue coveralls emerged from a wooden shack. He appeared to be no older than Ian, Felicia, and Lance.

"Y'all want it filled with regular or premium?" he asked Ian.

"No, thanks. Neither," Ian said. He gestured toward Felicia, who was sprawled across the rear seat. "My friend back there is pretty sick."

Felicia managed a feeble wave.

"Sorry 'bout that," said the attendant. "You want a Mello Yello? The bubbles make me feel good."

"Um, no," Ian replied. "We'd like to get her to a doctor, actually. How do you get to the nearest hospital?"

"My dad usually takes me," said the attendant.

Ian stared up at him for a moment.

"Well, how would *we* get to the hospital? Right now. By ourselves. Since we don't have your dad."

"Well, my dad's around here someplace. Just a sec." He raised two fingers to his mouth, then unleashed a piercing whistle. A plump red face poked out of the entrance to Woody's deli.

"Yeah? What's the matter?"

"These folks need a hospital. There's a sick girl in the back there."

The plump red face was attached to a stubby, rounded physique. It trundled out of the deli toward the Creature. The man wore a densely stained apron and a faded T-shirt that might, at one time, have read WOODY'S.

"I'm the owner of this establishment," he said. "Can I help y'all?"

"Oh, you're, um . . . Woody?" Ian said hesitantly. The man nodded.

"Great. Wow. Well, that's just great. This is really something, what you've built here. All this." Ian smiled. Felicia flung open a rear door and began heaving again.

"Woody, can you help us get to the nearest hospital?" asked Lance.

Woody leaned against the Creature. His face was inches from Ian's. His breath and skin reeked of beer.

"Well, take a right on 114, back at the big gorilla there," he said. "You'll go 'bout ten minutes down the highway and turn left at Dickson Road. It ain't marked, but there's a signpost there that used to have a sign that pointed toward the clinic. You can't miss it. It's a pretty big old post." Woody belched. Felicia heaved again. "Then you'll turn right after 'bout two more miles. Again, there's no sign. But there's a bait shop there. You can't miss it, either. The Boone County Clinic's gonna be on the right after another mile or so."

Woody stood up straight, then itched and patted his prominent belly. Felicia puked again.

"Thanks so much, sir," Ian said. Then he dropped the Creature into drive and pulled away.

"Y'all need a sandwich?" called Woody. "Some muffins, maybe?"

Ian waved again, turned right, and sped off.

Woody's directions were flawless. After a few minutes of frantic driving past the signpost, the bait shop, and very few other signs of human activity, the Creature screeched to a stop in the clinic's spacious parking lot.

Ian helped ease Felicia out of the backseat. She was cold and pale.

"I'm soooo lucky you didn't have football practice today, Ian. Or a big game. Big stud, you." She laughed softly.

"Save your strength," he said. "Because when you feel better, I'm kicking your ass."

Ian and Lance each flopped one of Felicia's limp arms over their shoulders, supporting her on the walk to the clinic's automatic door. As they stepped inside the large single-story building, underneath a sign that read, EMERGENCY/URGENT CARE, they were hit by a wave of cold air from an overhead vent and the startlingly loud strains of a country song from an overhead speaker. They approached the reception desk, where a young nurse's assistant sat behind a complicated phone and an array of clipboards.

"Can I help you?" she asked, smiling.

"Yes," Ian began. "My friend needs hel—"

Lance interrupted, dropping Felicia's arm and sweeping in front of Ian to address the pretty girl.

"Our friend's been puking cheese all over your fine state. It's been pretty gross. We think it's food poisoning," he said. "And hello. I'm Lance."

The nurse's assistant was an attractive green-eyed brunette in a strangely snug uniform. Her plastic name tag read, LINDA. It was clear to Ian where this was going.

He lightly shoved Lance aside.

"We really need to get her in to see a doctor," Ian said. "As soon as possible." Felicia's arm slid down his shoulder. She squeezed his hand.

"Sure thing. You all must be the kids Woody called about," said Linda. "I'll just need you to sign in and get registered." She handed Lance a clipboard, smiling, then extended a pen and a packet of multicolored forms toward Ian.

"Good old Woody," said Lance.

"Do you have an insurance card, miss?" Linda asked Felicia.

"Um, no," she answered. "Is that a problem?"

"Nope. Can't guarantee you won't get a big fat bill from the clinic, though." She grinned again.

"How soon do you think we can see someone?" Ian asked.

"Oh, not too long," Linda answered. "But like you can see, there are other folks waiting, too." She gestured toward a vast waiting area where all manner of sick and mangled persons sat quietly, thumbing through six-month-old magazines. A few runny-nosed children played with a collection of ragged-looking toys.

"Oh my," said Ian.

Felicia sighed, exasperated and ill. Ian took her by the hand, tucked the forms under his arm, and led her to an empty chair. Lance lingered behind to chat. Or whatever.

As Ian sifted through the pile of pages, he realized just how many details, both essential and mundane, he knew about Felicia Ruth Alpine. He filled in her address, her date of birth, her allergies, her parents' names, their places of employment, and their daytime contact information. In fact, he wrote for several minutes without asking her any questions. She rested against his shoulder.

"This is just frightening," he finally said.

"What?"

"All this crap I know about you. I'm wasting valuable brain capacity on this stuff."

"Such as?"

"I know Roger Alpine's home and work numbers. That just isn't right. It's like we're married."

"Wow." She grinned. "Imagine. Mrs. Ian Lafferty. That's about all a suburban girl could ever hope for. And pretty soon you'll have a wealth of lovemaking experience to bring to our marital home. I can't hardly wait."

"Wiseass."

"Isn't there something in that stack of forms you don't know?"

"Let's see. . . . 'Has the patient had gonorrhea?' Check. Syphilis? Check. Big scary genital warts? Oh, hell yes. Check." Ian mockingly patted Felicia's hand. "No, it looks like I've got it all covered. Nothing for you to worry about."

"Great. I'd hate to see you underrepresent my sexual history. I've worked so hard to attain it."

They laughed. Felicia continued to lean against Ian. After a quiet moment passed she said, "You know I've really never done it, right? Had sex, I mean. I've had boyfriends, as you know. But I've never treated sex as casually as guys seem to." She sighed. "I mean . . . well, it's no small thing, Ian."

Ian continued quietly leafing through the forms. It was strange, he realized. Felicia was one of his best friends, but he'd always just sort of assumed she *had* had sex.

"Oh, here's a question I can't answer," he finally said. He then pretended to read directly from one of the clinic's documents: "'Why the hell did the patient go to homecoming with Joey Swain in 2003? The Boone County Clinic still can't believe that shit.'"

"It says that?"

"It does, yeah. I swear."

"Really?" She laughed. "It says 'can't believe *that shit*'?"

"Yup. Right there. On the pink form. Really. Have I ever lied to you?"

"No, not since . . . oh, not since yesterday afternoon, I guess."

Ouch. That stung a little.

Felicia nestled against him.

"You're very comfortable, Ian. As a furnishing. You don't look like you'd be comfortable, but you really are." She pressed herself against Ian's rather long, ill-defined left arm. He brushed the hair from her eyes.

"Thanks. My rock-hard upper arms aren't too firm for you, are they? Not that I could do anything about it if they were. Since they're so rock-hard. Even when I'm not flexing."

"No, not really. Actually I'm not really detecting any arm-firmness at all. None whatsoever. You're more like an old pillow." She paused. "We fit very well together, Ian."

He thought for a moment, trying to decide whether that was the opportune moment to say something meaningful, heartfelt, and comforting, or to say something crass, lewd, and sarcastic. Then a stocky nurse with a manila folder in her hands burst through a set of swinging doors.

"Merle Dickey," she said in a stern voice. "Is Merle Dickey still in the waiting area? Merle Dickey, please."

A haggard man in a white undershirt and gray sweatpants stood up slowly, then walked toward the nurse. His right hand was heavily bandaged, and it appeared that a piece of dinnerware—possibly a knife or spoon, thought Ian, but most likely a fork—had been forcibly lodged in his palm. A police officer accompanied Mr. Dickey.

"What happened to you, Merle?" asked the nurse. "That looks un-comfortable."

"Minor domestic altercation. Vera just snatched up the fork from my bean salad and jabbed it right throu—"

They disappeared behind the swinging doors.

"Ouch," said Ian.

"Oh God," said Felicia. "We're quite a ways from home."

We're quite a ways from Charleston, too, Ian thought. Not that it mattered at the time. Ian felt more than a little responsible for coaxing Felicia to come along on the drive, and he felt more than a little awful for deceiving her at multiple points. And, what's more, he felt guilty somehow for not sampling those damn popovers, instead allowing Felicia to ingest every bit of whatever gut-rotting protozoa lay hidden in the cheese.

"Ian," she said. "I think I need you to get me a trash can."

He scrambled for the nearest waste container and rushed it over to her chair, just in time to catch another round of zooking. Well, most of another round, anyway. A few stray flecks of purged matter found their way to Ian's T-shirt.

"Sorry," Felicia mumbled.

"Oh, don't be. It's no great loss, this shirt. Just something random I picked out. Something I just thought might give me the best chance to have sex today. For the first time. Ever. In my life. That's all." He smiled. "No biggie."

"I'm sure the Internet skank would have appreciated your thoughtfulness."

"Yeah, that's what I've always heard about Internet skanks. They like subtlety."

"Have you seen Lance lately? Speaking of skanks," Felicia asked.

"Nope. Don't expect to see him, either, until he's bored with Linda. Or unless your nurse is incredibly hot. Then he might reappear."

The swinging doors flew open again. A different nurse with a different manila folder scanned the waiting area, then called out, "Nancy Hilgendorf? Nancy?"

An older woman in way-too-tight polyester pants and a floral-print blouse stood up not far from Felicia and Ian. She smiled in their direction. As she passed by, she bent low and whispered to them.

"I can remember the morning sickness, dear. Not my favorite part of pregnancy, but we all go through it!" She beamed at Felicia, who heaved again. The woman chuckled, shuffling along toward the nurse.

Ian giggled. "You should've told me you were pregnant," he said. "I would've given you at least two additional pee stops. I'm not so heartless." Felicia swatted at him blindly, keeping her face bent over the trash can.

"How could you possibly have anything left to throw up?" Ian asked.

"Dunno. But I did have quite a few popovers." She coughed. "Ick. My mouth is dry. My head's pounding. And I'm cold. And my stomach *hurts*, Ian." She sniffed.

He wrapped an arm around her. "You're dehydrated. Let's maybe try to steer the conversation away from your stomach, okay?"

"Okay. Then let's talk about Danielle."

Ian didn't feel much like talking about her, either. Somehow it was easier to justify this trip—and the sex that was supposedly waiting for him at the end of it—when he wasn't around Felicia. She muddled things. Even when she wasn't harping on him about the hypersexual depravity of the trip, she reminded him through the ease with which they interacted that he enjoyed no such rapport with Danielle. It wasn't that he didn't like Danielle. He did. She seemed fun enough. But to her, Ian was an inconsiderate (yet socially viable) football-playing stud. And he was aware of this fact during all of their interactions.

And his awareness of this made it impossible for him to ever relax or establish even the most rudimentary of real connections. Everything was affected by the fact that if she knew who he really was, she probably wouldn't be wasting her time on him in the first place.

If Ian admitted any of this to Felicia—if he even discussed it out loud—he risked losing whatever validation he derived from the relationship with Danielle (even though he had no right to that validation, as her continued interest only validated an absurd collection of lies). He'd be left exactly as he viewed himself: awkward, romantically inept, and more or less ignorable.

So discussing Danielle with Felicia was a complicated thing.

"Do we have to talk about her? Couldn't you just tell me about some deeply underground European pseudo-punk band I've never heard of? I like when you do that."

"You shouldn't have sex with this girl, Ian Lafferty."

He was silent.

"And you shouldn't try to be the guy who gets girls by playing them. It's shitty, it's phony, and it's not you. And anyway, you'll get all the wrong girls that way."

"You mean I'll get the *hot* ones that way? Because that's the way it seems to work."

"No, dumbass, I mean you'll get the *wrong* ones. You'll end up with girls who *need* to get the brooding, mysterious asshole guy in order to boost their basically nonexistent egos. You'll end up with the sort of girl who defines herself by who likes *her*, not by what and who she actually *likes*. You'll get other girls like Danielle, who won't ever notice, or even care, if you're being real with them or not, because they're not interested in *you*—they're only interested in how you make them feel about themselves. And it won't mean a thing." She jerked forward. "Oh, shit."

She heaved into the trash can, although it seemed she finally had nothing left to heave. For a lengthy moment, Ian still said nothing. He again swept back the hair from Felicia's face.

"But whatever," she continued. "If this is what you want, fine. I just thought you were different from the standard-issue sex-crazed boy, Ian."

Ouch. Ian Lafferty, defend thyself.

"I *am* different. A little different, anyway. I mean, I'm still a teenage guy. 'Sex-crazed' comes with the territory. It's not my fault."

Okay, that was weak, he thought. He began to feel defensive and unsure. In some ways, he felt that pursuing Danielle was simply what he, as a seventeen-year-old boy, was *supposed* to do.

"So you're a victim of hormones?" asked Felicia. "Of biochemistry? What? Please tell me."

More dry heaves.

"Something like that, I guess. Look, I began things with Danielle just wondering if I could make the whole Lance approach work. It wasn't some conscious decision to become a total jerk in order to scam with every girl I could get my paws on. It was—"

"'An experiment,'" she said. "I remember. And don't give me that crap about Lance. I love Lance like a brother—a nasty, scheming little shit of a brother—but he's not quite where you are on the maturity curve, Ian. And he doesn't have one approach—he has, like, an unlimited number of approaches, based on the girl, the setting, the time of day, the weather . . . whatever. God only knows what he's saying to this Linda chick. He's just a horny dude. *Love* isn't really a factor for him, I think. It's transitory. I didn't think you were like that."

"Jeez. What do you *want* from me?"

"I don't know, Ian." She shook her head, looking at the ground.

The stocky nurse reemerged. "Felicia Alpine," she said. "Is there a Felicia Alpine here?" Felicia stood up and walked quickly and unassisted toward the swinging doors.

Ian was in no mood to concede the last word to Felicia, so he followed her toward the nurse. Good thing, too. Dizzy from dehydration, she stopped suddenly and began to wobble. Ian caught her just before she could fall into a large arrangement of plastic flowers. The group of sniffling children tittered at her near-collapse. Ian shushed them.

"Oh my," Felicia said weakly. "Thanks, Ian."

"No problem."

The nurse took Felicia's arm. "You don't look so good, child."

"I've felt better," she answered.

The nurse led Felicia and Ian to a small examination room, then pulled a yellow curtain around them for privacy. Felicia explained that the likely cause of her nausea was a platter of old—potentially *very* old—cheesy popovers. The nurse asked her a series of questions, took her temperature and blood pressure, and handed her a paper-thin blue gown.

"Put that on, honey. The doctor will be in to see you. There's a bathroom just down the hall if you'd like some privacy. The boyfriend can wait in here while you change," she said.

"Oh, this isn't my boyf—"

The nurse ducked behind the curtain and stomped away. Felicia held up the gown.

"*Gawd*, I hate these things," she said. "Why do they have to reveal so much butt?"

"The hospital-supply industry is known to be controlled by pornographers. You're so naïve, Felicia."

"Guess so." She slouched on the exam table. "Listen, Ian, I'm sorry to beat you up over this Danielle person."

"No, you aren't."

"Okay, so I'm not. Because I'm right. But I'm trying to be magnanimous here. And I don't want to get you mad at me. I just want you to think it through." She paused, then sighed. "This is certainly not how I thought we'd be spending the last summer weekend before school starts."

She moaned plaintively, balled up the gown, and slid down from the table.

"I guess I've gotta change. Please step outside for a moment while I slip into this buttless garment."

Ian lifted back the curtain and found himself near a nurse's station that appeared to be the busy nexus of the clinic's urgent-care center. Phones rang, doctors barked instructions, nurses made unreadable notations on dry-erase boards. Ian stood quietly along the outskirts, making an effort to get out of the way of everything until Felicia poked her head out of the exam room and beckoned him to return.

She sat demurely on the steel table, attempting to pin the blue gown beneath her legs to guard against butt slippage. "You're sick, you're tired, and they put you in this thing that clearly wasn't intended for three-dimensional people. So demeaning." She exhaled loudly. "I miss my damn dog." Felicia looked completely drained. But she always had an unaffected cuteness to her, too, Ian thought.

Unprompted, he snatched a tongue depressor from a large glass jar, grabbed a pair of latex gloves from a metal dispenser, and plucked a rubber band from a collection of hepatitis pamphlets. He quickly bound the items together, then, grabbing a black marker that had been affixed to a biohazard bin, he drew a smiley face on an end of the tongue depressor. He then tossed the ad hoc creation to Felicia.

"Like it?"

"Sure, Ian. What is it?"

"It's supposed to be a dog. Since, you know . . . you miss yours. The gloves are its ears."

"But where are its paws? And the tail?"

"Yeah, tragic backstory with that dog . . . "

She smiled and patted the dog on his flat wood head. "Woof," she said. A knock came from just outside the curtain. Felicia placed the odd dog-thing on her lap. Seconds later the curtain whooshed back and the physician entered. She was youngish and wore thick glasses. No fewer than four pencils jutted from the bun of hair atop her head.

"Hi, I'm Dr. Eggelston. So you're Felicia, yes?" The doctor spoke fast, and in a decidedly un-Southern accent. She didn't wait for a reply. "Bad cheese, I hear. That's lousy. I love cheeses. May I ask where you encountered it?"

"Bodner. Is that right, Ian? Bodner?" He nodded. "Bodner, Indiana.

At a friend's house. Old cheesy popovers. They were actually pretty tasty. They had a light flaky crust, an ample portion of cheese. Not bad. I couldn't stop eating them. Now I can't stop throwing them up."

"So you kids are on the road, eh?" The doctor peered into a file folder, reading something with apparent interest. "That's nice. Off to college? Eloping, maybe? Escaped from prison?" She looked up at them. "I'm joking. I'm sure you aren't convicts. Police contact us about that sort of thing." She looked back at the folder. "So let's see. Vomiting, no significant fever, cramping . . ."

The doctor conducted a short examination, re-asked all the nurse's questions, and agreed that it was probably food poisoning and that the popovers were the likely culprits.

"So do you prescribe something? Does she get checked in to the clinic? What happens?" asked Ian.

"Sorry, doctor," said Felicia. "My friend here is in a hurry. I'm inconveniencing him quite a bit right now."

"I'm *concerned*," he said forcefully.

"Not much else happens, actually," said the doctor. "In all likelihood, she stops throwing up very soon—if she hasn't already—and she begins to feel much better. Probably within two or three days. Her stomach might still be a little queasy. She won't want to be too daring in her food choices. She needs to stay hydrated, drink clear fluids—this is a big deal."

Ian nodded. He was deeply relieved. But, almost immediately upon learning that Felicia wouldn't go the way of Lance's mom's cousin's friend, he felt the urge to get back in the car and scream down the interstate as fast as the Creature could safely go.

"So we're okay to leave?" he asked.

"Well, we do like to get a blood test to learn what bug is causing the symptoms. I don't really think we're dealing with something too strange here. Nothing she can't fight off. Probably a very common bacteria. But we're doctors, so we like to *know* things, not guess at them."

"Sure," said Ian. "Of course. Go for it."

"Maybe I'll just run this by the patient, too, okay?" said the doctor. Ian clammed up.

Dr. Eggelston addressed Felicia. "Does that seem all right, Miss Alpine?"

"Um . . ." Felicia had a rather ruminative expression, given that she'd been asked a question to which the only reasonable response, Ian thought, was "Yes." But she continued to waver. "Um . . . hmmm . . . I don't know, doctor."

Ian began to interject.

"Felicia, just take the bloo—"

She shot him a withering Shut-the-hell-up look. So he did.

"I don't think I can handle a blood test. I really can't. I'm already feeling so icky, and the sight of blood—especially *my* blood—well, I can't handle it. But I promise if things get worse I'll come right back to the clinic. Really."

"Felicia," said the doctor in a didactic tone. "It's standard. And we don't need gallons of blood, just a little. Your friend here will be by your side. I'm sure your parents will—"

"Oh, I think my parents are totally aware of my issues with needles and blood, doctor. Honestly. And you've made me feel much better already."

Ian observed that Felicia was attempting to appear as ruddy and bright as possible.

"Well, I can't *make* you submit to anything, Miss Alpine. But we take cases of food poisoning very seriously." She paused. "I hear you guys stopped at Woody's. You didn't eat at his deli, did you?"

"Oh no," said Felicia. "I wouldn't have chewed the gum there, doctor. No, it was definitely the very old popovers." She began to gather up her clothing.

"Okay, then. No more popovers for you. And remember: fluids." Dr. Eggelston handed Felicia a pamphlet on food poisoning, then flung open the curtain, jotting notes in the folder as she walked away.

Ian spun around to face Felicia.

"What's *with* you?" he asked. "Shouldn't we make sure you don't have, like, a killer tapeworm or something?"

"What's with *you*, Ian? You know they need my mom and dad's permission for a test like that, right? Well, it's gonna suck enough when my parents get a bill from this little cat-shit box of a clinic. How am I going to explain *that*? I certainly don't need some doctor calling my dad right now and asking him if it's okay to check my blood for vermin. Hell, they might have already called them for all we know." She took a breath. "Anyway, *I* am not going to scuttle this little trip of yours. You'd never forgive me. While I certainly don't think you should have sex with the Carolina ho-bag, I'm also not going to be the reason you don't. Not like this."

She held up her jeans, examining them for puke splotches. "Now get outta here while I change. You probably noticed that at no point did the doctor or any other member of the hospital staff need access to my butt. What is *with* these gowns?"

Ian smiled, then exited the exam room and strolled aimlessly toward the nurse's station.

She's right about her parents, of course. She's no dumb cookie. What if the clinic has already contacted them? Good grief, that would sure suck. We'll have the state police after us. And Roger Alpine will kill me. Crap.

"Ian," called Felicia, "you'd better go find Lance." Ian spun around to face the curtain. "He could be anywhere and doing anything with that Linda. Or whoever else." Quite by accident, the exam room curtain had settled against the wall in such a way that Ian could see beyond it. "I'll just meet you in that waiting area out there someplace. I'll be easy to spot, probably bent over a trash can or a potted plant." He very clearly saw Felicia's reflection in a metallic towel dispenser. She was slipping out of the gown. "I think I can make it there without your help. I'll walk slow and cling to the walls." Ian looked away. Staring at her felt too surreptitious. But he'd seen enough to remember that—underneath her veneer of androgynous and oversize clothing—Felicia was a babe. Somehow he'd gone a long time without noticing.

"Are you out there, Ian? Say something." He didn't, not at first. He couldn't—at least not until he'd gathered himself back around the idea that Felicia was his closest friend, and that, together, they were traveling to Charleston so that Ian could have sex with a ho-bag. *No, that's Felicia's word. Danielle's not a ho-bag. She sent the sweetest IMs. Excellent use of emoticons. I'm pretty lucky to have fou—*

"Ian!?" yelped Felicia. "Are you out there!?"

"Yeah, out here. Right here. Sorry. Just got distracted. There was a, um . . . a cool medical thing."

"Well, now I'm dressed." She dragged the curtain back, still moving slowly. Her hand was pressed to her abdomen. "Ugh. I'm in so much pain. Think I could keep an Advil down?"

"No, probably not." Ian supported her by the elbow. She leaned into him. "We'll just take it slowly. Lance can't have gotten far. Unless there was a shift change among the nurses and he followed one home."

As soon as Ian and Felicia shuffled through the swinging doors, they saw him—and a few seconds before that, they had *heard* him. He was singing to the gaggle of children in the clinic's waiting room. The kids sat cross-legged, swaying from side to side. Lance sat in one of the waiting area's low chairs with an acoustic guitar on his knee. Ian was struck with a sudden moment of confusion. When had Lance learned how to play the guitar, and for that matter, where had he found one in a rural clinic? And when had Lance Nesbitt developed an interest in entertaining small child—?

Ian soon observed that seemingly every pretty young nurse's aide—and there were several of them—stood somewhere near Lance, clapping. Ian immediately recognized the song that he was performing—the Pixies' "Monkey Gone to Heaven," which Ian had no doubt introduced Lance to at some point.

"There was a guy
An underwater guy who controlled the sea"

Lance nodded at the kids and smiled. The nurse's aides beamed at him with completely unwarranted affection. Felicia laughed soundlessly. Ian stared at Lance, bewildered as his friend reached the chorus:

"This monkey's gone to heaven, this monkey's gone to heaven. . . ."

When Lance finished the song, the kids mobbed him. They begged him to sing another. The nurse's aides giggled, closing in around Lance in a tightening circle. *Incredible. He doesn't even like that song. He doesn't even own the album. And he sings like a sheep. Dork. He just knows kids like monkeys, and hot young nurse-helpers like kids.* Ian and Felicia waded through the thick mob and grabbed Lance by the arm.

"C'mon, Elvis," said Ian. "Time to go."

"But, um . . . doesn't Felicia need some sort of IV? Shouldn't she maybe spend the night? You know, for observation? Shouldn't she–?"

"No. She's going to be just fine. Let's go."

With that, Ian steered Lance away from his adoring fans.

"He's just so *sweet!*" said a nurse's aide. "I could eat 'im up!"

"Pweeze!" shouted a tiny boy. "Do the monkey song again!"

But Lance was halfway to the door. He paused briefly to return the guitar to a stout little man in mariachi attire. The mariachi was seated next to a moaning companion who had a black eye, swollen lip, and a gruesomely broken arm.

"¡Gracias, señor!" said Lance.

"No, señor," said the mariachi. "Thank *you.*" The man with the broken arm nodded.

"Unreal," said Ian.

"If we could've just stayed another hour, I *guarantee* I could've found a quiet little supply room where me and Linda and a few of her friends could have–"

"Oh, get over yourself, Lance," said Felicia.

"No, I'm serious. Nurses are freaks, dude."

"You're not enjoying the road trip, Lance?" asked Felicia.

"It's not bad," answered Lance, walking toward the car. "But Lafferty is kind of a buzz-kill." They exited the clinic and found themselves once again in the sweltering Southern sun.

The Creature's clock read 1:32. But, it occurred to Ian that they were on East Coast time. So 2:32. He changed the clock.

Lance was at the wheel. He had insisted upon driving in order to make up for his earlier transgressions. Ian might have objected, but his head was throbbing. A lack of sleep, the various stresses of the trip, and an abundance of wildly unhealthy food had worn him down. Besides, Lance had a reputation for driving inadvisably fast and with reckless precision. If you needed to make up time—which they did—Lance was your man.

The Creature peeled away from the Boone County Clinic, sending up a cloud of dust and dirt. The tires smoked. The car screamed down the lonely country roads, past the foreboding gorilla of Woody's hickish oasis, and back onto the interstate, where Lance veered ruthlessly through the afternoon traffic. The Creature's ancient engine sounded like a washing machine full of bricks, and Ian couldn't quite make himself take a peek at the speedometer. But they really were making excellent time.

With Lance focused on the highway, Felicia squirming with discomfort, and Ian scared for his life, the car's occupants had fallen silent. The only sounds were a CD playing on the car stereo—a mix Felicia had created of Chicago hip-hop and angry young Brits—the thunderous rattle of the car itself, and a few more gastronomical aftershocks from Felicia.

Ian began to calculate the time remaining on their trip.

Assuming infrequent stops and no diversions—we should spend approximately one hour and twenty-five minutes traveling through North Carolina. But Lance drives like it's a freakin' NASCAR tryout. So if I multiply the original estimate by a Nesbitt factor of, say . . . 0.85, then we're left with . . . oh, let's see . . . one hour and twelve minutes. And from the state line, it's supposed to take another three hours and fifty minutes to reach Charleston. Factor in Lance's maniacal ass-hauling and we have . . . hmmm . . . three hours and sixteen minutes. Not bad, really. No, not bad at all.

But Danielle hadn't written him in quite awhile. *Maybe she's given up on me. Maybe she should. Or maybe she's a little freaked, too.* He fired off another text message to Danielle:

> *slight* detour. very sorry. b there b4 8 pm.
> really I promise! :)

He hit send before he suddenly realized that, in his concern, he'd accidentally sent his last message as real Ian, not jerk Ian. Jerk Ian wouldn't apologize, wouldn't use exclamation points, and would certainly *never* use smileys. *Oh, crap. Stay in character. You'll be there soon.*

"We should be in Charleston by 7:39," Ian announced to his friends. "Give or take."

"Does that mean he can slow down?" Felicia asked. "Or does he have to keep this hell-ride going?"

"No slowing down," said Ian.

"I'll do my best, Captain Solo."

"Han Solo was actually a general by the end of *Return of the Jedi*, you know."

"And you," said Lance, "were the geekiest guy in the galaxy by the end of *Return of the Jedi*. You'll have to keep the sci-fi comments to a minimum with this Tastee-Freez chick."

On they drove, over rivers and past an almost unbroken line of state parks. Lance periodically complimented the Creature. In spite of her discomfort, Felicia invented a game to help pass the hours and ease their boredom. Whenever they passed a town with a sufficiently odd name, she composed a country ballad to celebrate it.

"Ooh, there's a sign up ahead. Goody. Let's see . . . 'Junaluska.' That's perfect. Hmmm . . . *My dog smells like poop and I just chugged a twelve-pack / I'm waitin' by the phone but ol' Lance ain't called back / I gave it up to him Thursday, an' now it looks like it's over / He left me drunk and broke in Junaluskaaaaa. . . .*"

"That's great," said Ian, clapping. "Another gem. You really have a gift for country music, Felicia. It's like you're a lost Judd sister or something. But maybe with a little more darkness and self-loathing."

"Thank you, Ian."

"Yeah, that was nice," said Lance. "But why am I always the redneck bad guy in these songs? Maybe I want to be the rugged, dreamy cowboy type that you—the female balladeer—is faithful to. I should be the big-belt-buckle ranch-hand dude that you're pining for."

"Hmm," she said. "I'm not feelin' it, Lance. Okay, here's another sign. . . ."

They traveled on, rocketing down I-40. They entered South Carolina almost precisely when Ian had predicted they would. He was quietly proud of this fact. Just as quietly, he was getting a little jumpy. There were no more state lines to clear, no more milestones. Until Charleston, that is. He sat fidgeting.

Felicia called home—ostensibly to check in with her parents, like any responsible daughter would, but mostly to see if the Boone County Clinic had contacted them to request permission for treatment. They hadn't, it seemed. At the very least, they hadn't spoken to Felicia's mother, who was busy weeding the flower beds when Felicia called. Her father was out golfing. She tried to sound as healthy and safe as possible.

"Are you having fun downtown, dear?"

"Yes, Mom."

"Glad to see your friends, I bet."

"Yes, Mom."

"So, school starts this week, doesn't it?"

"Yes, Mom."

"All righty, then."

"'Bye, Mom."

Click.

"No sense telling them about the popovers until the bill arrives," she said.

Ian called his father's cell phone, too. Larry and Deborah Lafferty were quite enjoying themselves in Vegas. Larry was learning about new polymer onlay techniques—"I tell you, Ian, some of these people aren't dentists. They're *wizards!*"—and Deborah was playing slot machines into the morning. All seemed to be going well, and no suspicions had been aroused. Lance declined the opportunity to call home. His driving style was not particularly conducive to cell phone usage, and, since he was supposed to be staying at his cousin's apartment, he was afraid that his parents might ask to speak with Doug. "And really," he said, "I'm just not the call-home type. I think my parents know it. They'd just be weirded out."

A line of dark clouds gathered to the west. Pleased with their progress, and still feeling as if he had a tiny prospector chiseling away inside his skull, Ian suggested that they stop for gas and fast food.

"Gas *and* food?" Lance asked. "Wow. You're feeling pretty generous. What have we done to earn such benevolence?"

"It's a risk, stopping. No question. Anytime we allow you to have sustained contact with women of any age—or species—we seem to find trouble. But we've been making good time and, well . . . I'm starving. And like you said, I have to be fit to perform."

"Excellent," said Lance.

"Gross," said Felicia. "I mean, both the thought of food *and* the thought of you performing. So gross."

They exited the interstate and headed west. Road signs had led them to believe that somewhere near Forkboro, South Carolina, they would find a variety of gas stations and food options. They wove along the surprisingly twisty two-lane road until they arrived at the cluster of strip malls and gas oases. Lance, suddenly overwhelmed by a desire for nuggets, parked the car at Chick-fil-A.

"Yay, processed chicken!" said Lance.

Felicia moaned. "Oh God. I don't think I can watch you guys eat that crap. I'll hurl in your dipping sauce."

"You should at least get something to drink," offered Ian. "Remember what the doctor told you. Fluids, hydration, et cetera."

"Okay, yeah, fine. But you guys have to promise to eat discreet. And without any icky slurping sounds. And—most importantly—no cheese." They stepped out of the car. It seemed that every time they did so on this trip, the air was thicker and hotter. By the time they stepped inside Chick-fil-A, Ian had already developed great circles of sweat on his T-shirt.

After receiving their trays of deep-fried chicken parts, Ian and Lance rushed to a table. Felicia lagged behind warily, not wishing to think about food, let alone watch people ingest it. She was skeptical that Ian and Lance would obey the "eat discreetly" portion of her earlier request—and her skepticism was warranted. They ate like cavepeople. She turned her back to them and sipped a Sierra Mist.

"So, Ian," she said, "getting nervous? Preperformance anxiety setting in?"

"Don't listen to her," said Lance, chewing. "Nothing to be nervous about."

"Well, Ian? You're not even a little uptight? C'mon."

Like you don't already know. He was, of course, uptight about the having-sex part. But Ian had also begun to fear not-insignificant differences between the Photoshopped pictures he'd sent Danielle and the smallish boy who would be showing up at her door, too. He felt no need to discuss it with Felicia, though.

"I'm just eager," he told her without making eye contact. "Let's just say that."

She leaned toward him.

"Why is this so important to you, Ian?" she asked.

"The sex?"

"No, your chicken, asshat. *Yes*, the sex."

"It's not just the sex," he said. "I wanna meet Danielle, too."

"And have sex with her!" Lance said with a grin.

"So what about the *sex*? Why is this such a big friggin' deal, Ian?"

"Dude," said Lance, lifting his head and staring at Felicia incredulously. "You're asking a high-school guy why he wants to have sex? That's like asking a clown why he honks his nose. It's just what we *do*."

"Just didn't think Ian was a clown, I guess."

The three sat in silence, listening to Muzak versions of Phil Collins songs.

It's not a terrible question, Ian thought. *Why sex? Well, for starters, it's sex. Not the sort of thing you refuse lightly.* Secondly, having it for the first time would be the sort of singular, momentous happening that might allow him to someday recollect this summer as not having been so crushingly dull. And yeah, maybe Ian felt a bit loserly, as if every other guy his age was up to things that he, in his dull and sequestered life, could scarcely imagine, like there was some secret sex-having universe from which he'd been excluded.

Lance and Ian soon finished eating. When they left the restaurant, the sky had grown darker. They quickly filled the Creature's gas tank at a nearby Shell station. With the dashboard clock reading 3:41, they began to pull away.

"With any luck at all, Forkboro should be our last stop before Charleston," said Ian.

He pulled the Toady out from beneath the passenger seat. Danielle had finally answered him:

```
8 pm? wtf?! go faster!
```

Seconds after that, she'd sent another:

```
. . . but when U get here, promise 2 go slow ;)
```

"Message from the girl?" asked Lance.

Ian said nothing. He simply showed Lance his Toady.

"I am a slave to the road."

Lance looked left and then right, preparing to steer the Creature back toward the interstate. Then a Jeep full of girls sped by the gas station.

"No . . . *way!*" said Lance.

His head swiveled around, tracking the girls. He stomped on the accelerator. Ian's car screeched onto the highway after sliding briefly on the dirt of the shoulder. Soon the Creature was pushing a hundred miles per hour, rapidly approaching the green Jeep.

They were traveling in entirely the wrong direction.

"What the *hell*, Lance?!" yelled Ian. "What the f'ing hell?!" Lance's eyes were glued to the Jeep as it hurtled down the two-lane highway. Ian continued yelling.

"Turn around! What are you doing?! Leave the girls alone, Lance."

"Ohhh," groaned Felicia, disturbed by the velocity of the Creature. "Sick girl back here. Hello?"

Lance said nothing. He remained fixated on the Jeep. It wasn't exactly meandering slowly through the Carolina backcountry. No, it was blazing, often cutting turns too sharply and slipping into the opposing lane of traffic. If there had actually been any traffic, this would have caused problems. But the road ahead was empty. The Jeep's three female passengers rode with their arms extended through the vehicle's open top. Ian thought it looked as if they might be dancing. Not that it mattered to him—he only cared about getting his own car turned around, and quickly. But Lance was wringing every shred of horsepower from the Creature's engine, steadily gaining on the Jeep while getting farther away from Danielle with each passing second.

"Lance, please! They have girls in Charleston, too—lots of 'em. Enough of them that even I managed to meet one. So *please*. I'm begging. We've gotta turn around."

"I don't think he can hear you, Ian," said Felicia. "He's in some kind of girl frenzy. Like sharks around fish entrails. He can't act rationally. He's like a superdeadly predator. I am actively freaked out."

The Jeep skidded, then darted down a gravel road. Its tires kicked gray dust into the air. Lance followed. The Creature shrieked as it turned.

"*That*," Lance finally said, "is no ordinary bunch of girls."

"Okay, so they were cute. Charleston has lots of cute girls!"

"It's not their cuteness, guys. Not that I'm *objecting* to their cuteness, but that's not it."

"So why the hell are we following them, Lance?!"

"I know the driver."

"You *what*?"

"I totally know the driver."

"We're in South friggin' Carolina, Lance," said Felicia. "We don't know shit in South Carolina, and you don't know that girl! It's about five hundred degrees outside. You're insane from the heat. It happens. So stop the damn car."

"I'm not insane." His right leg was fully extended against the accelerator. The Creature revved in protest. "And I *do* know that girl. I could *never* forget that girl." He paused. A nostalgic tint softened his voice. "That's Elise Millwood. We met in Missouri, at Birdeye Creek

Science Camp. We were thirteen. All we did was hold hands, but they were the best two weeks of my life!" He sighed. "And they were the worst. I *totally* blew it with her. Can you believe that?" He pounded his hands against the Creature's faux-wood steering wheel. "She was amazing. So cool. Scary cool. But I've always known that fate–or God, or Mark Burnett, or something–would bring us together again." Gravel clacked against Creature's windshield. The girls had stopped dancing and were instead staring back at the Creature with a combination of interest and disbelief.

"Of course, I didn't think I'd be reunited with Elise quite this *soon*," Lance continued. "Somehow I thought we'd meet when we were old. Really old. Like maybe in a nursing home. And we'd both reach for the same bowl of peas, or we'd get bingo at the same time, or we'd– Oh, shit."

The Jeep took a sudden left down a dirt road lined with tall trees. The girls were heading into a dark and worrisome forest. Lance tailed them, barely missing a giant pine. Branches scraped against Ian's door.

"Lance, this is crazy! You think a girl you saw for a split second traveling at eighty miles an hour through some backassward town is the *same* girl you had a crush on five years ago in a different state?!"

"Yup. At science camp. She worked magic with a petri dish." Thunder growled in the distance. "I'm not the dog you think I am, Felicia," Lance said. "I love that girl. Seriously. I loved her at camp, I love her now." His eyes didn't leave the road.

The Jeep made a series of turns down increasingly narrow roads– in fact, they weren't so much roads as grassy clearings that happened to have fewer trees than the rest of the forest. Ian looked at Felicia with a panicked expression. She pressed her face into the rear seat and began muttering.

"My God. This is so *Dukes of Hazzard*. I can't look. Wake me when we're dead, so I can kick Lance in the groin."

Lance was on the Jeep's rusted bumper. The girls were bouncing along the rough terrain, grinning back at Lance. He waved.

"I just need room to get alongside 'em, dude."

"No, Lance," said Ian. "That's just an incredibly bad idea—maybe the worst of your many bad ideas over the last day and a half. You've noticed that we're in a forest? With big, immobile trees? Not really a passing zone." He tightly gripped the handle on the door with his right hand and braced himself against the dashboard with his left. The Creature thumped along the grass. Lance stared hard beyond the Jeep, his face desperate and serious, looking for the slightest opening.

"I've gotta get up there. I have to talk to her. When Elise sees it's me, she'll— A-ha!"

They suddenly emerged from the forest onto a dirt road, which quickly became a paved surface that snaked along a small creek. The Creature stopped shaking quite so violently when it returned to asphalt. A cluster of mobile homes came into view. Although the road wasn't properly demarcated with a yellow center line, it was plainly wide enough to accommodate two cars side by side. Lance gunned the engine. The girls slowed, allowing the Creature to close the gap.

"Oh, man," said Lance excitedly. "I can't believe this is happening. Elise Millwood! This girl is special. She's incredible. Forget the other chicks I've messed around with." He shook his head. "This is the one. *The One*." He paused. "What the hell am I gonna say?"

Lance let the Creature slip back behind the Jeep.

One of the girls—a well-proportioned redhead in a tight lavender tank top, looked back and shrugged her shoulders as if to say, "You're quitting *now?*"

Ian stared at Lance with the same question on his mind. A few raindrops began to plunk lightly against the car.

"For cryin' out loud, Lance! Don't stop now, not after dragging us through miles of dirt and brush and muck! Do it! Get up there!"

"I don't know what to say. This girl is . . . well, she's very different from other girls."

The redhead was yee-hawing in the Jeep, gesturing at Lance and Ian to pull ahead. Felicia moaned in displeasure in the back of the Creature.

"You're Lance Nesbitt, dammit!" said Ian. "You don't need pep talks. You *give* pep talks. To losers like me. So get up there! Flash a little charm, do your thing."

Lance looked sincerely afraid.

"Or just tell her how you've always felt," Ian added.

"Right," answered Lance. "That's the move."

He accelerated again, and the Creature crept along the side of the Jeep. The redhead—as well as a curvy, gap-toothed blond wearing a terrifying amount of mascara and blush—yipped and screamed at the giant sedan as it approached. The back of the driver's head was visible now, her sandy hair pulled into a ponytail that flowed from the back of a baseball hat. The Creature drew closer.

"Tell her how I've always felt," Lance mumbled.

"Nothin' to it," said Ian. Under the typical Lance-chases-girl circumstance, Ian wouldn't have been so forgiving. But he felt a tug of empathy for Lance, watching him chase an unlikely second chance.

"Dude, you have to drive."

Lance released the steering wheel, unbuckled his seat belt, and rolled down the window. Ian yelped with fear, then grabbed the wheel and steadied the car.

"Scoot all the way over," urged Lance. He lifted his foot from the accelerator and eased himself halfway out the window. Rain hit his face. Ian flipped on the wipers. Lance balanced on the edge of the driver's side door, holding onto the roof of the speeding Creature. The Jeep girls continued their twangy hooting. There could be no slowing, so they hummed along at a steady sixty-plus miles per hour—after the hellish, breakneck ride through the forest, anything less than eighty felt almost pedestrian. Lance began calling out to the Jeep's driver. She was clearly smiling, enjoying the pursuit.

"Hey! Pull over!" The rain fell somewhat harder. Lance grinned, waving his arms above his head. "Enough already! Let's talk!"

The girls laughed.

"Well, ain't you a rowdy thing!" the redhead exclaimed.

Ian focused on the road. Felicia peeked briefly at the front seat, then buried her head again. She moaned feebly. Lance continued yelling above the rush of the wind, pleading with the Jeep's driver.

"Pull over! We have to talk!" He held his hands together as if in prayer. "*Please!* Don't you remember me?"

The blonde driving the Jeep finally turned to face Lance. She had a flawless smile, a deep brown tan, dazzling eyes. Ian glanced at her quickly. Lance continued to yell.

"Please pull over! Please! We *have* to talk! I've been thinking about you every day since camp, Eli—"

He stopped talking. The Jeep's driver looked at him quizzically.

Lance's mouth twitched, but no words came forth. Raindrops raced across his face. After a short sequence of stuttered noises, he spoke again.

"Never mind, girls. Um . . . it was nice driving with you. Thanks. Cool Jeep." With that, he plopped down in the driver's seat, squeezing between Ian and the door.

"My bad. That's not Elise."

"What?!" screamed Ian and Felicia in unison.

"We all make mistakes, people. Just chill."

The Creature decelerated. The Jeep sped away. Ian ceded control of the wheel to Lance, then slouched in the passenger seat. He sat in stunned silence. Only then did they notice the wailing siren behind them, and the red and blue flashing police lights.

"Oh shit, Ian," said Lance. "You weren't speeding, were you?"

A massive state trooper stood just outside the Creature, making a window-rolling gesture with his hand. Rain dripped from his wide hat and streaked down his mirrored sunglasses. Lance quickly lowered the window and addressed him.

"Afternoon, officer. What'd we do?"

"I need to see licenses from both y'all," said the trooper in a deep and possibly affected baritone. "I'll need this vehicle's registration, too." He bent low and peered into the Creature. "And I'll need 'em *now*, gentlemen."

Ian could smell the cinnamon Altoids on the trooper's breath. *That's considerate,* he thought, before completely falling into an un-tempered panic. His mind raced. *What's the absolute maximum amount of bad shit that this could bring? Jail, courtrooms, bail money, angry parents, prison food, cellmates . . . big, angry cellmates. Ack!* Ian's pulse leaped. Lance appeared weirdly calm as he dug his license from his wallet and handed it to the officer. But Ian's hands were shaking as he unlatched the Creature's glove box. He fumbled noisily inside the dark compartment. Disoriented by fear, Ian mistakenly grabbed several Dunkin' Donuts scratch 'n' win coupons and passed them to the trooper along with his license and vehicle registration.

The officer closely examined the documents produced by the occupants of the battered Creature. His face betrayed no emotion, nor any discomfort in spite of the rain. The trooper paused when looking at the doughnut coupons. He extended his hand and fanned them out, as if counting them.

"Is this supposed to be some sorta *bribe*, son?"

He peered into the car again, indignantly returned the coupons to Ian, and poked his large head into the back.

"Hello, miss," he said to Felicia. She nodded.

"Oh God," said Ian. "No. No sir. Not a bribe at all. And I'm not trying to insinuate anything—not anything at all—about cops and doughnuts. I think that's just a big, unfortunate myth. These were just in my glove box, that's all. They were with the registration. I'm, um, in the business." He paused. "The doughnut business. And believe me, my store is not overrun with cops." He chuckled nervously. "That just doesn't happen the way people think." Lance gave Ian a pained look, as though urging him to stop prattling. He didn't. "Of course, if you want the coupons, they're yours. You can have them."

The officer merely stared.

"But I'm not trying to bribe you, officer," said Ian. "Honestly."

"I've been offered a lot of things in my time on the force," said the trooper. "Money. Beer. Reefer. Favors from promiscuous persons. But nobody—not once—has offered me doughnuts in order to avoid getting a ticket. Please don't do that again." The trooper removed his head from the car and stood.

"Sorry for the misunderstanding, officer," said Lance. "My friend's wound a little tight right now. We've had a long trip."

The officer stared at Lance for a protracted moment, then looked at the licenses.

"Illinois, eh? Hmm. Illinois . . . " He let the word hang in the air. "They teach people to drive like that in Illinois, Mr. Nesbitt? With all that hangin'-out-the-window-driving-sixty-eight-in-a-fifty-five-zone nonsense? That was really somethin'. We don't usually drive like that in Union County."

"No. No, sorry, officer," said Lance. "It was completely unsafe. I know. It was more about the girls, sir. In the Jeep." The trooper stared at Lance. Or rather, it *seemed* the trooper was staring at Lance. The rain-speckled sunglasses made it impossible to say. Lance continued. "I thought I knew one of the girls, sir."

"But you didn't, I take it."

"No."

"Since that would really be an astonishing coincidence. You, a young man from . . ." He examined the license. " . . . *Naperville* runnin' into someone you happened to know here in the quiet Carolina countryside."

"Yeah, I was pretty amazed myself, sir."

The trooper removed the glasses, wiping the lenses free of rain, then looked into the Creature toward Ian.

"And that woulda been you drivin' the vehicle while your friend hung out the window?"

"Yes, sir. I drove. And I tried to keep it under fifty-five. But, you know . . . the Jeep was really driving erratically."

The trooper exhaled.

"Hmm. That Jeep seems to be a real source of trouble for you boys." He looked again into the backseat at Felicia. "You all right back there, miss? You seem a little frazzled. That musta been a helluva ride."

"It was not pleasant, officer, no." She belched. The trooper continued staring at her. "Excuse me," she said. "Bad cheese."

The officer stood, looked over the Creature from tip to tail, then said, "Y'all sit tight. I'll be right back." He strode back to the patrol car.

"Jee-*zuhs*," said Lance, looking exasperated. "You tried to give him *doughnut* coupons, Ian? Why not just call the guy a lazy pig and let him cuff you? I do *not* need to be jailed, Ian!"

"It was not intentional. And it was definitely not a bribe. I've just got a boatload of those stupid friggin' coupons in the car, that's all. They're all over the glove compartment." Ian paused. "And gimme a break, Lance. Don't complain to me. We wouldn't even be here in— where are we again? *Union? Forkboro?*—if you hadn't hijacked the entire trip in order to pursue a girl who, of course, was not the girl you expected her to be. I mean . . . *aaarrgh*."

"Oh, I am so not feeling well," groaned Felicia. "That whole race-through-the-woods thing? Not good on the old tummy."

"Sorry," offered Lance. "That was dumb. My bad."

The rain seemed to relent, and rays of sun glinted off the droplets on the Creature's hood. But a line of storm clouds waited ominously to the west. The three friends sat in contemplative silence for several minutes, waiting tensely for the trooper to return from his car. Then Felicia fell across the backseat, groaning again with a spasm of nausea, opened the driver's side door, and vomited every drop of her sixteen-ounce Sierra Mist onto the road. A few moments later, the trooper returned, carefully stepping over the pool of fresh puke. Lance rolled down the window.

"Looks like maybe your girlfriend in the backseat there can't handle her alcohol," said the trooper. "I wonder how much you've had."

"Honestly, officer," Felicia said forcefully. "I haven't been drinking. It really was bad cheese. I've been to see a doc—"

"Now, how many vomiting teenagers do you think tell me they *have* been drinking, miss?" The trooper paused, though the question had clearly been rhetorical. "None. Not once in my thirteen years and four months as a police officer has a drunk teenager admitted to being drunk. So here I am with some potentially chemically altered out-of-state kids driving crazy all over my roads. Hmmm. We *do* incarcerate people for such infractions, you know." He turned to Lance. "Have you consumed any alcoholic beverages, Mr. Nesbitt?"

"No, sir. And neither has she. It's the tru—"

"Please step outta the car, Mr. Nesbitt."

"But, sir, we really . . ."

The officer stood firm and expressionless.

"Okay," said Lance, opening the door and stepping onto the slick asphalt. Ian again stared at Felicia with wide, frightened eyes. She cupped a hand to her mouth in an effort to restrain another burp.

The trooper continued to look at the front seat of the Creature. He again removed his sunglasses, then ducked low to address Ian. "Mr. Lafferty, may I ask what *that* is?" He pointed toward the driver's side floor mat, where a piece of red licorice lay covered in fuzz and wrapped in a condom.

"It's a Twizzler, sir. In a prophylactic."

The trooper stared at Ian.

"I see," he said at last. "And in the state of Illinois, do they teach schoolchildren to practice safe sex with Twizzlers?"

"No, sir. They don't really say anything either way. About Twizzlers, sir."

The trooper kept staring.

"Is there any reason that particular Twizzler required protection, then?"

"No, sir. It was, um . . . it was part of a demonstration. Sir." *Oh shit, Ian. Just stop talking. Stop talking right the F now.* But he couldn't. "A condom demonstration, sir. By Mr. Nesbitt."

Ian could see Lance hopping with anxiety just outside the car. *Yeah, we're so going to prison. I don't think I can do hard time. Lance, maybe. Me, no.*

"I see," said the officer, standing to address Lance. "Well, Mr. Nesbitt, you do seem to have many areas of expertise. High-speed stunt drivin'. Girl chasin'. Condom application." The trooper walked around Lance slowly. "Let's see if maybe driving while intoxicated is one of your talents."

"But officer!" Lance said, half laughing. "I have *not* been drinking. At all. You can ask my friends—I really don't need alcohol to act stupid around girls."

"I'm inclined to believe that's true, Mr. Nesbitt. I really am. But seeing as how one of your passengers just tossed her cookies—no, 'scuse me, her *cheese*—on the road here, and this car reeks of vomit, *and* you were driving this vehicle in a most reckless and dangerous manner—an offense for which you may yet be cited—I'd like to ask you to submit to a field sobriety test, Mr. Nesbitt. If you refuse to submit to this test—"

"No, sir. I'll take the test," said Lance. "I really haven't been drinking. Truly. It's just, well . . . " Lance glanced at Ian. "I've been making some very poor decisions lately. As I think you've pointed out."

In the crushing Carolina heat, the trooper proceeded to direct Lance through a series of tests that, it seemed, were designed to do little more than make the person being tested look as foolish as possible. Lance walked heel-to-toe along a straight path on the side of the road; he balanced on one foot and counted slowly for half a minute; he stood perfectly still and focused his eyes on a small metal object that the trooper held aloft. "Follow the stimulus, Mr. Nesbitt," said the trooper.

Lance did.

"I'd be happy to take a Breathalyzer test too, officer. I seriously haven't had a thing to drink. I know a lot of people tell the police that they've just had a couple beers or whatever. But honestly, sir, I haven't had anything. Not a drop."

"Well, Mr. Nesbitt," sighed the trooper, "either you are the most coordinated drunk I've ever encountered, or you're being honest with me. Which I certainly appreciate." He gestured toward the car. "You may reenter your vehicle."

"Thank you, sir."

Rain began to fall again. Ian felt slightly more at ease.

"But don't let that young lady in the backseat drive this car, Mr. Nesbitt."

Felicia thrust a handful of papers from the Boone County Clinic out the window toward him.

"I really did eat some bad cheese, sir. Back in Indiana. I was treated for food poisoning not long ago. I've thrown up in maybe three states so far." The officer took the papers. He seemed to soften a bit as he reviewed them.

In what Ian thought was a remarkably fortunate outcome, all things considered, the trooper decided merely to issue Lance a ninety-five-dollar speeding ticket and a citation for not wearing his seat belt. He also delivered a terse lecture about the perils of pursuing pretty girls on the winding back roads of South Carolina. After awkwardly lavishing the trooper with thank-yous, Ian asked him for assistance in returning to the interstate.

"Aw, that's real simple," said the officer. He then described a rather convoluted path back to the highway that involved a series of numbered rural routes, a right turn at a septic tank (or was it a left?), a llama ranch (or were they alpacas?), a T-intersection near a water tower (or was it a Y near a water *park*?), and something about a Long John Silver's that had closed in 1979 (or maybe it was a Red Lobster in '89). No one took notes. They all just kept saying, "Uh-huh," and nodding.

After the trooper returned to his car and sped off, Ian declared that Lance was forbidden to drive for the remainder of the trip. Lance happily relinquished any behind-the-wheel responsibilities. Just as Ian turned the key in the Creature's ignition, the rain began to fall in blinding sheets.

"We're so lost," said Felicia glumly.

"No," said Ian. "Lost is what we were five minutes ago. Now we're doomed. We're toast. We're finished. We're like those cattle skulls you always see in cartoon deserts. We're like Von Dutch hats. We're over. We're *dead*."

"Dude," said Lance. "Don't you think that's maybe a slight overreaction?"

"Oh, listen to the guy who got us into this friggin' impossible mess. He says I'm overreacting. Overreacting! It's Saturday night, Lance. I'm supposed to be having sex. But instead, I'm . . . well, I can't even see where the hell I am."

That much was true. For nearly twenty minutes, rain had hammered the car and obliterated the view through the windshield. Lightning crackled all around as the Creature inched steadily along the lonely, rural Carolina roads. They encountered exactly none of the roadside landmarks they'd been told to look for. They certainly hadn't encountered the interstate. They were, in fact, way past lost.

"That cop's directions sucked," said Lance. "This whole state is sucking so far. Improper signage on the highways. Girls who look like people they aren't. Too much rain."

"Is that something up ahead?" asked Felicia. She pointed toward a yellow speck of refracted light.

"Maybe," said Ian. "Or it could just be another car. It could be anything."

The wipers slammed back and forth noisily, accomplishing nothing. They drove slowly toward the golden speck, watching it steadily grow. After several anxious seconds, it became identifiable as a backlit sign. It read, simply, ELMO'S. Neither the sign nor the structure—a one-story white building with aluminum siding and only a few small windows—offered any indication as to what goods or services Elmo might provide. But they didn't care. They needed help. Ian parked the car directly in front of the entrance and the three friends dashed inside.

Despite the fact that no more than eight feet separated the front end of the Creature from doorway to Elmo's, their heads were soaked with rain when they burst through. Much to their astonishment and delight, Elmo's was a clean, air-conditioned restaurant. The walls were lined with pennants, plaques, and black-and-white photos that celebrated the glorious past of some football team or other. A plump middle-aged woman seated at a nearby booth quickly stood up, patted her impressive bouffant, and walked toward them briskly. She wore a pink apron, brown half-stockings, and a white waitress uniform.

"Goodness, look at you poor kids," she said amiably. "You're soaked clean through." She withdrew three menus from behind a hostess's podium and smiled. "Smoking or non?"

"Oh," began Ian, "we're not here to—"

"Nonsmoking please," said Felicia firmly. She grabbed Ian's hand. "We should get directions and wait the rain out, Ian. No more blind driving. No more looking for right turns at septic tanks or whatever else. You guys sit and have something to eat. Maybe coffee. I'll sit and feel like cold poo."

They followed the waitress to an empty booth. In fact, all the booths were empty. So were the stools at the counter. The only occupants of the restaurant were Ian, Felicia, Lance, their waitress, and a dreary old grease-splattered man with a horrid combover in the kitchen who was, in all likelihood, Elmo.

"You kids want anything to drink while you look at the menu?"

Ian and Lance ordered coffee. Felicia asked for water with a lime wedge.

"No limes, honey," said the waitress breezily. "The Ritz we ain't." She flounced away. The rain beat loudly against the restaurant's windows.

Ian scanned the walls. His eyes landed upon a large antique relief of a leather-helmeted football player. The player was carrying a ball, and inside the ball was a small clock. Ian rose and took a few steps in its direction before stopping.

"Good God," he said. "It's already after five o'clock." He shook his head. "I'm done. Finished. This was a brave, misguided attempt. But it's clearly not happening." He slouched in the booth, then allowed his head to fall onto the laminate tabletop with a thud. Lance began to jostle him.

"C'mon, Ian. The situation isn't that bad. We're not all that far from Charleston, right? Didn't you say we'd be there at, like, seven-thirty? So we're a little late."

"We're already a *day* late, Lance. For a visit that's only supposed to last two days. And I have to be at work in thirty-six hours. And that doughnut suit has regurgitated popover on it. I'm so done. *Done.* Dead, dead, dead."

"That's no way to talk. The rain will let up, the sun will shine, we'll get back on the road, and by nine o'clock—ten at the latest—this Danielle chick will be rushing to the car to greet you. Nude, probably."

"Because everything has gone just that smoothly so far," said Ian bitterly.

The waitress brought their drinks.

"Y'all know what you wanna eat?"

"Bacon," Lance said happily. "I'd like a plate of bacon, ma'am."

"Nothing for me," said Felicia.

"I'd just like toast," said a gloomy Ian. "White bread, please."

"Dude!" said Lance, bumping Ian's side with his elbow. "You've gotta *perform*, remember?"

"Oh, are y'all some kinda entertainers?" asked the waitress.

"Sort of," said Felicia. She gestured toward Lance. "This fella here is an actor." Then she looked at Ian. "My other friend is a football player. And I guess I'm something like a cheerleader."

"How nice," said the waitress.

"Ma'am, you'd better bring my buddy here a side of bacon, too." Lance grinned. "He's got a really big game tonight–his first one. Ever."

The waitress looked down at Ian, who was still slumped over the table.

"Kinda scrawny-lookin' for a football player, aren't you? Must be a punter or something."

"Exactly," said Felicia. "You guessed it."

The waitress strolled back to the kitchen. Felicia laughed softly while Lance slurped his coffee and erected a pyramid from single-serving containers of half-and-half.

"I suppose we'll make it there tonight," Ian said into his place mat.

"That's the spirit," said Lance.

"Yay. Woo," offered Felicia. "Havin' sex with a total stranger. Don't wanna pass that up, Ian." She slid out of the booth and stood up slowly. "I'm going out to the car to get my toothbrush. I've decided I'm not throwing up anymore. It's time to freshen up."

"Get my Toady, will you?" asked Ian.

Felicia frowned. "Need to check in with the Web floozy?"

"Something like that." He tossed Felicia the keys to the Creature, then collapsed deep into the contoured ass-groove of the booth. He sighed.

"The bacon will perk you right up. The protein. It energizes you. I've read about this."

"The fat will congeal in my veins. I'll collapse dead."

"Or that. Whatever." Lance faced Ian, then leaned in close and spoke in a near-whisper. "Dude, this isn't good. You're too down, too mopey, too worried. It's like you've turned this beautiful thing into just another item to tick off on the ledger of Ian Lafferty's life achievements: 'Honor roll, perfect attendance, new high score on Halo, sex with hot college girl . . .' That's messed up. Now, I'll admit that I may have presented a few unnecessary obstacles on this trip . . ."

Ian scowled.

" . . . and I'm sorry about that," said Lance. "Really. But Ian, you should still be psyched. There's still time. You just seem so—"

"Worried. I know," said Ian. "I can't shake it."

"Well, what the hell are you so worried about? You've played this perfectly, dude."

The entrance to Elmo's flew open, jingling a strand of bells attached to the doorway. In racing to the car and back again, Felicia had resoaked her hair and T-shirt. She held a toothbrush and toothpaste in her left hand and Ian's Toady and keys in her right. Her sandals squished as she plodded toward the booth.

"Still raining?" asked Lance, smiling.

"I do not enjoy being soggy." Felicia dropped the Toady and keys on the tabletop, then squished off toward the restroom.

"So," Lance said, turning again toward Ian. "We've established that you're worried. About what, exactly?"

"What's *not* to worry about? There's presex small talk to get through. Any number of things can go wrong there. I've never even met the girl, after all, and she thinks I'm this totally other guy. Then there's the make-out/undress/foreplay thing. God knows what goes on there—I certainly have no idea. Then there's putting on the condom. I have to seem smooth and experienced, and I have to conceal its mangoness. Not easy. And then there's the sex. Where do I put my hands? What noises do I make? What if she doesn't make any noises? Wha–"

"Okay, dude. I don't need the *full* blow-by-blow. Um . . . so to speak. That was a fine summary. My advice is simple: Don't think, Ian. Don't overanalyze it."

"Oh, sure. Sounds easy. 'Cause when would I ever do that?"

"We're wired for this, Ian. All of us. Nothing is as natural. Billions of years of evolution, et cetera. If sex were difficult, we'd all be trees. Or somethin'. Anyway, you'll *know* where to put your hands, and you'll know where to put everything else. And if something goes weird, who the heck cares? That's the *real* beauty of this whole trip. There are no repercussions. Zero. Nothin'. Because with this girl, you haven't been yourself. You're not Ian Lafferty, doughnut boy and loser sci-fi geek."

Ian scowled again.

"Sorry. I mean, that's not to say that I see you that way. Exactly. But what I'm saying is, with this girl you're another person altogether. You're Ian Lafferty, Northwestern football stud. And by Monday morning, Danielle will be literally hundreds of miles away. Out of your day-to-day life. So no matter what happens tonight–you drool all over the sheets, you wet the bed, you cluck like a chicken, whatever–it's not like you'll have to see her at school on Monday. There's no pressure here."

"I suppose you're right," Ian said, staring idly at his flatware.

"Except there's maybe just one thing you need to consider," Lance added. "Not *worry* about. Just *consider*."

"What?"

"You want it to last a while, Ian. The sex, that is, not the relationship." Lance developed a somber expression. "There are certain things you do *not* want to hear from Danielle after you do it, like, 'Oh, this happens to lots of guys, Ian.' Or 'That's it, Ian?' Or 'I've had sneezes that lasted longer and felt better, Ian.' Those are bad phrases. The codas of disappointing intercourse. But there are techniques you can use to avoid those phrases."

"You're talking about avoiding premature ej—?"

"Don't even say it. Don't start thinking that way. It's not a mechanical thing at all. It's psychological. So keep it outta your kitchen." Lance tapped an index finger to his temple. "Don't let the thought get in there, dude. You'll develop bad habits."

Ian eyed him skeptically. "Where do you get this total *shit*?"

"I'm an avid reader."

"Of what? *FHM*? *Maxim*? *Jugs*?"

"I read a variety of publications, Ian. Some scholarly, some less so. And I think I have a little bit more experience in this area than you."

"Okay, then. By all means, tell me how I can avoid the problem whose name we dare not speak."

"You've got to think about something totally antisexual. Something that will help you prolong the act. A person or object from which you derive no pleasure. Fix it in your head. Otherwise, you'll be finished before she really starts. That's no good. Then she'll say the things you don't wanna hear. You'll be apologizing, she'll be consoling you—it's bad. You never want to find yourself being consoled at the end of sex. So you focus on something else while you're doing it."

Ian laughed. "I'm supposed to try not to enjoy it?"

"Ian, you're gonna enjoy it no matter what. You'll enjoy it if she farts and sings Christmas carols. For a guy, there's no such thing as *not* enjoying it. It's sex. What you're trying to do is restrain the enjoyment a little."

The waitress placed two plates on the table, each containing three slices of bacon.

"I'll be back with your toast," she said. The rain against the window seemed to lessen. Ian waited for the waitress to get sufficiently far away.

"And how do *you* restrain the enjoyment, exactly?" he asked.

"Me? I think about your dad. That might not work for you, though."

Ian recoiled and leaped from the booth as if he'd been Tasered.

"Aww, gross!" he yelped.

"Problem with your bacon, son?" asked the waitress.

"Oh no, ma'am. Just a problem with my friend here. Sorry."

Ian sat back down. Lance shrugged. The toast arrived.

"Dude, he's Larry Lafferty, my *dentist*. It's perfect. Your dad represents pain. Male authority. That weird latex glove smell. I can go nine, ten minutes just thinking about your dad drill—"

"Yuk! Stop!" declared Ian, waving a hand in protest. "Enough of today's lesson. Seriously. That's gross, man. I can't handle any more."

Felicia plopped down opposite them, setting her toothbrush on her napkin.

"What the heck was *that*?" she asked.

"You don't want to know," snapped Ian.

"I was just telling Ian that I think about his dad—you know, with the dental implements and the fluoride—so that I can last longer during sex."

Lance smiled. Felicia seemed unmoved.

"Yeah, I can see that," she said. "I didn't need to *know* it. But sure, I can see that."

Ian furiously spread butter and jam on his toast. Lance dangled a piece of bacon from his mouth like a pipe. Felicia took small, delicate sips of her water.

The waitress returned to their table to refill their coffee cups.

"Y'all need anything else?"

"No, ma'am," said Ian. "Just the check. Oh, and directions back to the highway if you don't mind. We're a little lost."

"Honey, if you're here and you ain't *from* here, you're lost. The interstate's only about three minutes away. Just go back the way you came 'bout two hundred yards. There'll be a llama farm on your left—that's Elmo's, too. He breeds 'em. Anyway, it's easy to spot." The three friends stared at one another. "So turn there at the farm, go another mile or so, then a left at the stop sign. There's an old Long John Silver's right there. Can't miss it. That'll take you straight to Highway 26."

She scribbled on their check for a moment, then dropped it on the table. Ian picked up the Toady.

"Chatting with the lady friend *again*, Ian?" asked Felicia. "Don't forget to say that, like, your punting foot hurts or something. Maintain the illusion."

Yes, that's exactly what I was going to do.

"No, I'm not going to chat with her. Just checking . . . other stuff."

Ian toggled idly through the photos on his Toady. The beach shots of Danielle were interspersed with pictures of Felicia from her prevacation bon voyage bash. Danielle looked serious, posed, and sultry; Felicia looked loopy, candid, and unpredictable. In one of the pictures she was posed with the tip of her finger in her nose, smiling goofily.

"Are you really ready to *be* this other guy, Ian? This asshole guy?" Felicia leaned across the table. "I mean, it's one thing to be all jerky and call a girl 'Tasty' in, like, an IM. It's another thing to actually talk that way. To a live person." She took another sip of water. "I guess Lance has it mastered, though."

"The way I act is probably the least of my problems," Ian said, shaking his head.

"What do you mean?" said Felicia.

"Well, you guys saw the pictures. I don't look anything like that."

Felicia and Lance stared at him blankly for a few awkward seconds. Then Lance grabbed the Toady from his hands.

"No, Ian. You didn't!" said Felicia, still sipping.

Oh. So maybe they missed the Photoshopped pics. But how could they? Crap. Damn, damn, damn, damn . . .

Lance pecked at the keys of the Toady and soon began laughing. Loudly. He tilted the screen toward Felicia, who immediately did a spit-take onto Lance's half-and-half pyramid. The small white containers scattered to the floor. Ian vividly recalled the details of the image that they were no doubt looking at. It was a rather flattering shot of him taken the previous spring at a Cubs game, but still not suitable for distribution to Internet babes in its unaltered form. So before sending it to Danielle, Ian had enhanced it. He'd added a dark brown tan and tamed his long, typically disheveled hair so as to make it appear short, excessively styled, and slick. And he'd given himself a goatee.

"Dude!" exclaimed Lance, in a voice loud enough to attract the attention of both Elmo and the waitress. "You are soooo *screwed.* When you get to Charleston, Danielle's going to think that Ian Lafferty sent his little brother to have sex with her!" He stared at Ian. "Huge mistake."

"I thought you guys saw the pictures already. When I was sleeping."

"Nuh-uh," said Felicia. "Your e-mails were entertainment enough. We never got this far." She looked at him. "A goatee, Ian? You don't even shave. And you've never been tan. *Ever.* All you do is burn and get all red. Like a giant radish. And you haven't had a decent haircut since fourth grade."

"Well, that's why I couldn't very well send her an undoctored picture. Again, I never intended to actually meet this girl."

"*Ian!*" said Felicia. "You *are* meeting her. But there's no way she'll recognize you."

"Dude, you're done," said Lance. "Hope is lost. I mean, I can tell you what things to say, and I can give you a little technical advice. But *this* . . ." He shook his head and looked at the screen. "This I can't do. You need a makeover."

"From a talented stylist," added Felicia.

"And we're in the middle of nowhere." Lance paused. "You are totally screwed."

They sat in silence for a few seconds. Ian thought through the predicament and began to think his friends might be right. But he, like Lance and Felicia, couldn't begin to think of a way to address the problem. Then the waitress walked toward their table.

"'Scuse me," she said. "Did y'all say you needed a stylist?"

It turned out that Elmo was not his family's only entrepreneur. His sister Lorraine was the proprietor of a beauty shop, which she operated out of a converted trailer on Elmo's farm. "Ladies come from miles around just to have Lorraine set their hair," the waitress had said, tapping her hand lightly atop her stiff tresses.

"Oh, that's lovely," responded Ian.

Elmo placed a call. Yes, his sister would open the shop. Yes, she was happy to give a makeover to a nice young Northern boy. "Looks like you're in luck," he growled.

Ian didn't feel especially lucky.

He drove down the winding dirt path that led past grazing llamas to the trailer-turned-salon. It had previously been Ian's opinion that he could compensate for any deficiencies in his physical appearance by overwhelming Danielle with attitude. The online persona he'd crafted was certainly brash and decisive enough to pull it off, he thought. But Felicia seemed insistent on the makeover. "You have to give this girl what she's expecting, Ian. It might even be fun."

"But you're always telling me that girls aren't as visual as guys," he'd protested.

"That doesn't mean we're blind, Ian. This chick thinks you're some kind of sporty meathead with a killer tan and a trendy haircut. So that's what you're going to be."

Ian parked his car in front of the trailer. A small cardboard sign on the screen door read OPEN.

The door creaked as they entered. The salon was a bright place with a low ceiling and a shiny orange linoleum floor. It smelled like hairspray and cigarette butts. A woman, presumably Lorraine, sat on the lip of a shampoo basin. She was small, wiry, and wrinkled, perhaps in her mid-fifties. She had a purplish growth on her neck that was about the size of a Jujyfruit. She was sipping Budweiser from a can.

"Welcome!" she said, striding toward them. "You must be the folks Elmo called about. Sit down, everyone, sit down."

She ushered them onto a low vinyl bench that sat opposite three ominous-looking hair dryers—the kind that lower onto a person's head and emit a terrible noise. As a little boy, when Ian accompanied his mother to a hair salon, he'd always imagined that such dryers had the capacity to switch peoples' brains. He had liked to pretend that the person coiffing his mother's hair was, in fact, an evil scientist and that he, Ian Lafferty, was the only person capable of stopping their insidious brain-flipping experiments. He'd once gotten yelled at in a crowded BoRics for unplugging a row of dryers and interrupting—apparently at some critical juncture—his mom's trans-formation into Courteney Cox. Ian flashed back to the incident as he scanned the room.

Lorraine lit a Winston, sucking in her cheeks like some great fish as she inhaled. After several seconds, she expelled a cloud of gray smoke with a hiss.

"So," she said. "Who needs the new hairdo?" She eyed each of their heads, gazing hard at Ian. "I'm guessing it's you. Well, I can smooth things up a bit and we'll have you outta here by six o'clock."

"Oh, that'd be great," began Ian. "We really need to get go—"

"Ma'am, I'm afraid my friend needs something more than a hair-cut," said Felicia. "Ian, show her the picture."

Reluctantly, Ian set the Toady on his lap and found the image. Lorraine stared at it for a moment.

"I'll be damned," she said in a whisper. "I'm just a country stylist, not a plastic surgeon."

Thank God for that.

"There has to be something you can do, Lorraine," pleaded Felicia.

"Well . . ." Lorraine paused, shutting her eyes and crinkling her face. "I did just get a trial shipment of self-tanner. But I don't have fake beards." She eyed Ian. "Aw, hell. Let's scrub him up a little and see what we get. Hop in the chair, honey."

She led Ian to a plush swivel chair, snapped a black plastic cape around his neck, and pulled a pair of long silver shears from a drawer. She took a few practice snips at the air and walked slowly around Ian.

"The first cut's always the toughest when you're losing a big batcha hair," she observed. "Here goes."

Lorraine descended onto Ian's head and began to cut. Long tendrils flew to the floor with quick, dexterous flicks of her scissors.

Felicia held up the Toady, examining the images while Ian fretted.

"I think what Ian was trying to create here was a crispy little flip-do. Where the bangs pop up and they're frozen with some kind of ultrahold gel. I'm almost positive. Is that right, Ian?"

He shrugged. "I guess. Maybe. I was just trying to look not so shaggy. Like a plausible football type."

"Well, that flip-do look is so over, anyway," said Felicia. "And the guy in this picture is a slave to trends. So I think we have to go with whatever hairstyle the contemporary American asshat jock boy is favoring these days. Maybe we should try a fauxhawk—like a mohawk, but without completely shaven sides. Can you pull that off, Lorraine?"

"Hell, there's really nothin' I can't do if you give me a good head of hair and a tub of pomade. So let's try it."

Lorraine kept snipping. The hair fell.

Ian sat still. *Ron will be happy no matter how dorky I look.* "The food service industry is no place for the long-haired man, Ian." *Thanks for the tip, Ron.*

Lorraine switched from scissors to electric clippers.

The clippers began to buzz. Ian felt them tug at his hair. Lorraine drank her Bud and took the occasional drag off her Winston. Felicia sang along with a Scorpions song playing on a tape deck. Lance leafed through magazines, sometimes singing, too. Increasingly smaller pieces of Ian's hair fell to the ground. He grew tense. His head felt significantly lighter. Without the shaggy curtain that once enveloped his face, he felt exposed. Felicia stood only a few feet away, grinning.

Lorraine said, to no one in particular, "I'm texturizing with the razor."

"Mmm-hmmm," said Ian.

She sang, drank, smoked, and cut. Then, laying down all cutting implements, she dipped her fingers into a jar of pomade, wiped her hands together, and began massaging the strong-smelling stuff into Ian's hair, pulling the follicles toward the center of his head. In mere seconds she was finished. She spun Ian around to face the mirror. Felicia stood over one shoulder, still grinning.

"Not bad," she said. "You'll be like the cool mysterious new boy at school, Ian. Until everyone figures out that you're the same old geek with hip new hair."

He examined his reflection from all sides. A large fin of hair ran down the centerline of his scalp. It didn't move, yet it didn't look too plastic and Lego-like, either. *It's really not bad,* he thought. *Not at all. For a half-drunk chain-smoker, Lorraine's very good.*

"You think Danielle will approve?" Ian asked Felicia. She seemed to wilt slightly.

"It's hard for me to get inside the head of your Internet ho, Ian, but I imagine this is closer to the look of the guy she's expecting."

"You mean the guy she was expecting *yesterday*?"

"Yup, that."

Ian began to rise out of the swivel chair. Felicia placed a hand on his shoulder.

"Oh no, my friend. You aren't finished."

Felicia turned toward Lorraine. "Do you think you can do something about his eyebrows?"

"What about my eyebrows?"

"Mmmm," said Lorraine. "I can see what you mean." She lit another cigarette. Felicia stood in front of Ian and ran a fingertip over his forehead.

"You have this tiny trail of hair that extends over your nose. Right now you're like a younger version of some old Soviet dictator. Or a Muppet."

Lorraine was soon smoothing a layer of hot wax over Ian's left eyebrow with a fine-bristled brush. He grimaced. "I swear you've got some of the prettiest, longest eyelashes I've ever seen," she said. "I know a lotta old ladies around here who'd kill for those."

"He does have nice lashes," said Felicia, leaning over Lorraine's shoulder. "You're absolutely right. Ian has some very lovely features. It helps having that mop of hair outta the way, too." She smiled.

Ian cringed as Lorraine passed the brush above his eye once more. "Hold still now, darlin'," she said.

The bright orange tip of her Winston flared and faded. She placed the brush on the workstation, then pressed a thin strip of muslin atop the hot wax on Ian's face. After waiting a moment, she began to peel back a corner of the strip ever so slightly. "This part here can sting a little bit," she warned. "One . . . two . . ." Lorraine's eyes widened. "Three!" She removed the strip from his face with a firm tug. In the brief interval between the horrible ripping sound and the onset of the searing pain, Ian realized that someone was calling on his Toady.

After he stopped yowling in hairless agony, Felicia flipped it to him. He quickly answered, neglecting to check the caller ID.

"Hello?"

"Hey, Ian." It was a female voice with a soft Southern lilt.

"Um . . . hello. Who's this?"

"Who do you *think* it is, silly. It's Danielle."

"Oh. Um . . . hey." He paused, deciding to drop his voice half an octave. "Hey, Tasty. Whassup?"

Felicia rolled her eyes and turned away. Lance perked up, scooting to the edge of his chair and smiling.

"Where *are* you? Are you really coming?"

Ian felt his pulse quicken. He had never actually heard Danielle's voice, a fact that he considered one of the more remarkable aspects of the whole Internet-girl-agrees-to-sex thing. It wasn't like she'd never tried to call him. No, she'd done that periodically over the past week. But he never answered. This casual disregard, he thought, made him more of an enigma. It also made Danielle seem a little less real to him, which made it easier to carry on with his assorted deceptions. But suddenly, with her cloyingly sweet voice in his ear, he felt awful.

Think of the beach pictures . . . the beach pictures. . . .

"Hell, yeah, I'm coming, Tasty. I'm just a few hours away, I think. We stopped to wait out a storm."

"We?"

"I mean *me*. I. Me alone. People say 'we' sometimes when referring to themselves. I do it all the time. We do it." He laughed awkwardly. Lance shook his head while Felicia snickered. "*I* stopped to wait out a storm, Tasty. A bad storm. With lightning and everything."

He spied himself in the mirror. His unwaxed eyebrow appeared significantly lower than his waxed eyebrow, freezing his face in the expression of a TV detective who'd just deduced something.

"Why do I feel like you're bullshitting me?" she asked.

"I don't know. Maybe because you're way too suspicious. Go look at the Weather Channel, freak."

"Okay, Ian. I'll believe you. But you've gotta get here quick, baby. I'm leaving for Spain."

"I know, Tasty. Monday night. But this is only Satur—"

"No, Ian! My daddy upgraded my ticket, but he had to change the date. So now I'm leavin' tomorrow morning. Early. And my sorority sisters are throwing me this party tonight, and . . . well, it feels like you an' me just aren't—"

"Tasty, I'll be there. I swear. I'm leaving now. Really. I can't wait."

Oh, crap. Real, nice-guy, reassuring Ian was coming out again. Too nice. Definitely too nice.

"Okay, Ian. I can't wait eith—"

Click.

Ian looked from Lorraine to Lance to Felicia. His eyes were wide—the left one looked somewhat wider.

"Okay, um . . . crap! We have to go, Lorraine. How much do I owe you?"

"Honey, you have *got* to get the other eyebrow finished up," she replied.

He looked at the mirror again.

"Okay," he said. "We do the eyebrow. Then we go."

She repeated the procedure on the right side, drawing another injured shriek from Ian. When Lorraine finally released him from the cape, he leaped off the chair and slid on the scattered clippings from his own head. He paid hastily, tucked the Toady in his pocket, offered his sincere thanks, and accepted a complimentary sample of self-tanning lotion. It was 6:16 P.M. when they left the salon/llama farm and headed for the interstate.

#

Felicia drove, despite suffering from frequent waves of queasiness. Ian was firm in his commitment to Lance's banishment from the driver's seat, so Lance lounged in back. Ian sat in the front, gazing at his new hair in the Creature's mirror.

"It freaks me out a little, this hair," he said. "It doesn't move. No matter what I do." He swished his head from side to side. "It's unnatural. Like having a hat growing out of my head." Ian lifted himself closer to the mirror, nearly pressing his face to the glass. "These eyebrows are kind of weird, too, huh? I look so . . . awake. Like I've had too much sugar. Or like I've just been badly frightened." Ian raised and lowered his eyelids, trying to mitigate the effects of the waxing.

"Oh, it's fine," said Felicia. "You had old man brows anyway, Ian. Now you just need to apply your tanning crap, and your makeover will be *finis.*"

Ian lifted the small jar of self-tanner that Lorraine had given him. He read the label aloud: "'Tan-in-a-Can self-bronzer: Easy to apply!

Fast-acting! Quick-drying! Scientifically formulated! Vitamin infused! The sun's own rays in a travel-size can!'"

"Dude, it's 'scientifically formulated,'" said Lance. "What could go wrong?"

"'The sun's own rays,'" repeated Ian. "I mean . . . wow. All the power of nuclear fission in this little jar. What *can't* science achieve?"

"Put it on, Ian," urged Felicia.

Ian twisted the jar's lid until it popped. He stuck a finger into the saffron-colored goop. He wiped it on his neck, then removed his T-shirt. Felicia hooted mockingly as the shirt came off.

Lance squinted his eyes and raised his hands to cover his nose. "Wow, that stuff *reeks*."

"It does have a certain pungency," said Felicia.

"But you guys both wanted me to look like the guy in the photo, so—"

"*Your* photo, Ian," Felicia reminded him.

"Well, whatever. I've only got a couple hours left to make the change. So this is how it has to happen."

Ian began applying the strong-scented goo to his pale legs and arms. Then he placed a large dollop on his belly and smeared it over his torso. Felicia and Lance both rolled down their windows and turned their faces toward the influx of fresh air. After several minutes of careful application, Ian extended the jar toward the backseat.

"Lance, put some of this gunk on my back, please."

"Oh, no." He shook his head. "No, that's not reasonable."

"C'mon, Lance," said Felicia. "Put some tanner on your friend. You *know* you want to."

"Just get the middle of my back. I can reach my shoulders."

Lance sniffed the jar tentatively. "*Damn*, dude. Two words: *Old. Dog.*" Lance dipped a finger into the goo, then placed it lightly on Ian's back just below his shoulder blades. He looked at Felicia. "No wisecracks, please."

"Wisecracks?" she asked. "You're just two handsome young lads applying lotion to each other. Is this what it's like in the boys' locker room?" she asked. "Guys just rubbing ointment all over other guys? Maybe exfoliating one another? Because that's what I've always suspected. That's what happens in the girls' locker room, you know."

"Oh, you can't tease me like that," said Lance. "I've had enough interludes in girls' locker rooms to completely demystify them."

"*What?*" Felicia asked, laughing.

"Heck, yeah. Some girls are totally into it. It feels a little dangerous. There's a kind of thrill. A possibility that you'll get busted by some old rat-faced gym teacher."

"Like which girls are 'totally into it,' exactly?"

"Oh, let's see. Well, there was Tracey Wong after softball practice last spring. And there was Carolyn Mueller during a basketball game. That was pretty sweet—she seemed a little out of my league. But, you know, sometimes you surprise yourself. Isn't that right, Ian?"

"Sure, Lance. Make sure you get my sides, under my arms."

Lance continued.

"Hmm . . . who else? There was Julia Carpoulis."

"Oh, that hardly counts," said Felicia. "Everyone gets it on with her."

"Hey, I don't do background checks. I don't make judgments, and I don't ask too many questions. I just take whatever opportunity presents itself."

"Still, that's quite something, you and Julia. Probably the two sluttiest people in the Chicago metropolitan area hooking up. What are the odds?"

"Pretty good, actually," said Ian. "How could they possibly miss each other?"

Lance finished applying the tanner, then scraped the excess from his hands onto Ian's neck. "Let's see," Lance said. "I know there must be a few more. Oh yeah . . . Deborah Kindred! It was between seventh and eighth periods one day last year. It was just before Christmas break, I think. Nothing major. A mutual grope, that's all. It was the holidays, everyone was in a good mood. And there was Lori Ambrose. Was that last year? No, sophomore year, I think. But my first girls' locker room encounter was Stacey Stichman. Remember her?"

"Wasn't she, like, a grade above us?" asked Felicia.

"Two grades, actually. We were in junior high. She was in eighth grade, I was in sixth. We'd both just finished serving detentions."

"You guys didn't, like, *do it*, did you?" asked Ian. "I mean, in the locker room. You were in sixth grade, for cryin' out loud. It's more than five years later, and I still haven't gotten close to having sex."

"Ah, but that's about to change." Lance grinned. "And no, I didn't *do it* with Stacey Stichman. Not then. No, it wasn't until like three years later, after—get this—another detention. Funny how things come full circle."

"Sometimes you amuse me, Lance," said Felicia, her eyes on the road ahead. "And sometimes you just totally give me the willies. This is one of those willies times."

Yuk, thought Ian, smearing tanner onto his shoulders and neck.

That just isn't right, all that intercourse and near-intercourse. Especially in locker rooms. That much messing around is icky. Too icky. Is it ickier than what I'm about to do? I think so. Maybe not by several orders of magnitude, but it is definitely ickier, no question. Ian dabbed his right pinkie into the Tan-in-a-Can, then carefully covered his face and ears with the noxious stuff.

"So Lance," said Felicia. "Ever do it with a girl in a *boys'* locker room?"

"Nope. I haven't taken a girl into a boys' locker room for the same reason I haven't taken a girl into a slaughterhouse. Or a Porta Potti. Or a landfill. Because that's friggin' *disgusting*."

They laughed. A few miles ticked away as Ian began to dry and darken.

"My God, Ian," Felicia eventually said. "That junk really does stink. Which means *you* kinda stink." She turned her nose away.

"Sorry," he said. "Maybe the smell will fade after a while. Otherwise I'll have to find something to counteract it. I'm afraid to put my shirt back on. It might get in the fibers."

"We'll have to wash you off somewhere," Lance said.

"Let's just try to give it another hour or so to take effect. We want me tan, right?"

"Not if it eats away your skin," said Felicia. "The fumes might make us hallucinate. I think I'm getting lightheaded. That could also be popover-related, of course."

"We just need a new topic," Ian said. "Something to distract everyone from my smell."

"Felicia, how 'bout you share with us stories of your sexual misadventures," said Lance. "*Something* must've happened in Europe, right?"

"Well, I did get hit on a little. It was flattering. The Mediterranean boys really like the Americans, I noticed. But no real misadventures. Some very provocative dancing in clubs, that's all. And a near-interlude with a boy named Jacques. But nothing much happened. It's tough to sneak away from your parents and scam on foreign boys."

"Prude," said Lance. "Girls like you never give it up."

"*What?!*" Felicia squawked. "'Never give it up'? Well, no. I haven't given it up. But I don't know that I'm a *prude*."

"Joey Swain said you were a prude, dude."

"*What?!*"

"After homecoming. He said he got nothin'."

"I am *discerning*. That doesn't make me a prude. I'm not specifically trying to save myself for marriage or prom or anything. Who knows? If I met the right boy, I might be a freak."

"Hmm," said Lance, pretending to consider the possibility. "No, I can't see it. Not a girl like you."

"What does that even *mean*?" she huffed. "A girl like me? Tell me please, what am I *like*? Ian, do you know what I'm like?"

"I'm staying so far out of this conversation. I'll just be over here stinking like old dog."

"Oh, just chill, Felicia," said Lance. "I didn't mean it in any sort of bad way. I just meant girls who don't have many girlfriends. You hang out with guys—you hang out with me and Ian. Girls like that, they tend to be a little more prudish. Um . . . as a group."

"I have girlfriends!" she declared. "They may not be my *best* friends, but I have them."

"Okay, name one."

"There's Tanya Turcott. She's a good friend of mine."

"She moved away freshman year."

"We still talk," Felicia said, unconvincingly. She thought for a moment. "And there's Beverly Gishblatt."

"She was a student teacher sophomore year."

"Peggy Swain?"

"Dude, that's Joey's mom."

"Chris Puddleman?"

"Chris is a guy."

"He's very effeminate."

"You kicked his ass in third grade, remember? You thought he took your fruit roll-up—which he didn't—so you gave him a beatdown with a cafeteria tray. That was awesome."

"Okay, okay. So I do not currently have many girlfriends. It's not like I don't *like* girls. And I've actually been quite girly at many points in my life. You don't think I was totally into My Little Pony? Or Strawberry Shortcake? Or Jem and the friggin' Holograms? Well, I was." She paused. "It's just tough to maintain a friendship with some girls. They have needs. Lots of needs. They get all teary-eyed about boys. They like to talk about themselves more than I care to listen. It's just easier with you two."

"Hey," said Lance. "You're preachin' to the converted here."

"And besides," she added, "I can't remember ever not knowing you guys. Other kids, they move into town, then move away. They enroll in school, then they leave. But you guys have always been around. I'm very attached to you. Some people you're stuck with." She smiled. "Even when they lie to your face about some online skank."

After that pronouncement, the miles passed in relative silence for a time. Ian's smell began to dissipate. When the goo completely dried, he put on his T-shirt again. The sun slipped beneath the tree-tops. The distance to Charleston began to appear on road signs. Ian grew increasingly apprehensive. He also grew increasingly orange. Lance was the first to point this out.

"So you're not exactly turning *tan*, are you?"

"What do you mean? I'm darker." Ian examined his forearms.

"You look like a carrot stick," said Felicia, erupting in a laugh that she'd been holding in for several miles.

"Mmm-hmm. It's more like orange sherbet, though," said Lance. "But the basic point is valid. You're pretty friggin' orange."

"Nuh-uh," said Ian. But objectively, he recognized that it was true.

"Maybe you're still changing color, dude. You could still get a little darker."

"I don't know," said Felicia. "It's been almost two hours. I think he's fully cooked."

"You think it's really that bad?" asked Ian.

His friends merely nodded.

"Well, um . . . what can I do?"

"Maybe you can wash it off," Lance offered.

"I'm thinking the time to wash it off would have been, oh, I don't know . . . *two hours ago!*" Ian twisted in his seat, staring out the window to the west, then slammed his hand against the dashboard. He flipped open the mirror on the passenger side's sun visor and began to closely inspect his reflection.

"I seriously *cannot* believe you guys talked me into this. I mean,

I'm not sure that Danielle would have been into me the way I looked, say, this morning. But come *on*. This is a bit more of a risk, don't you think?"

He wheeled around to face Felicia, orange-skinned and fin-haired, his unnaturally slim eyebrows arched like a McDonald's sign. She began to laugh again, and this time without restraint. The Creature briefly drifted onto the shoulder of the interstate. Felicia quickly straightened out the car but couldn't recompose herself nearly as easily.

"Glad I can entertain you," Ian said glumly.

At an exit that couldn't have been more than ninety minutes from Charleston, near the little town of Dognall, Felicia pulled the Creature off the interstate. Before Ian could protest, she announced, "Pee break!"

Sullen and humiliated, Ian sank lower into the passenger seat.

"You thought I forgot about my pee breaks, didn't you?" Felicia asked. "Well, I didn't. Never give a girl an advantage and expect it to go unused." She pulled the Creature into a Sinclair gas station and dashed for the restroom as soon as they were parked at a pump.

Lance placed a hand on Ian's shoulder.

"I'll fill up the Creature. You try to get your head in a better place. Here's the thing: orange though you may be—and strangely groomed—you are, right now, looking a little more like the guy Danielle is hooked on. And she *is* hooked. She wouldn't call begging to see you if she wasn't. So just chill."

He exited the car and began to fill the tank.

Ian looked into the mirror again. *What the hell am I doing? Who is this? That's one orange-lookin' dork, that's who. Shit.*

Ian sighed.

"Maybe I'll get something to try to mask the scent," he said.

"Now you're thinking tactically. I like that, Ian. Um . . . not that you need to hide your scent. Lots of women find 'old farty dog' to be *very* hot."

The fragrance options inside the Sinclair were limited. Ian could either purchase an incredibly small travel-size bottle of Old Spice for $5.99, or he could get a package of three tree-shaped car air fresheners for $2.29. He went with the Old Spice, but not without hesitation. He also purchased a Milky Way, a one-liter bottle of Mountain Dew, a "Big Grab" bag of Doritos, and a pair of sunglasses to at least partially obscure the alterations to his brows. He sulked back toward his car, determined to drive the rest of the route himself.

Okay, so it's just after eight P.M. I can still make it before ten if we can avoid any additional delays. But not even one more thing can go wro— Hey, where the hell is Lance? Uh-oh . . .

Ian tossed his provisions onto the hood of the Creature, then walked briskly back into the Sinclair. Much to his surprise, Lance had not affixed himself to any girl(s) but was instead simply waiting in line to purchase a Dr Pepper and a box of Bugles.

"Did you think I'd run off again?"

"No. Well . . . maybe. Possibly. You must be kept on a very tight leash until we reach Charleston, that's all. Then maybe you can roam a little."

"Yeah, let's discuss Charleston," said Felicia, who'd sneaked into line behind them. "What exactly do you expect Lance and me to do while you're, um . . . *doing stuff* with the Internet sex kitten? Like, where are we supposed to sleep? Evidently not at Danielle's place, since you decided not to tell her about us—a weird move, by the way. Are Lance and I supposed to just sit patiently in the car while you two have sex?"

"Would you? Because that would be great."

"Dude, we'll find a place to stay," said Lance. "Just relax. It's a big city, lots of rooms, and we all know you've got your mom's Discover card, Felicia. Anyway, we might just wanna stay out all night. We'll cruise the nightlife, sip fruity drinks. Charleston's an old city, probably full of cute Southern lasses."

"I have to sleep tonight, Lance," said Felicia. "Sick girl here, remember? We were at the hospital, like, a few hours ago. Here's an update on my condition: still puke-ass sick."

"Dude, you haven't blown chunks since that cop who thought you were totally wasted had you all freaked out. And if I recall the events at the clinic correctly, the doctor's only instruction was for you to drink plenty of *fluids*. No one said anything about sleep, and I'm sure no one told you not to have any fun. So let's just get to Charleston, get Ian situated, and see where the night takes us, okay?"

"Not that I haven't mentioned it before," Felicia said, "but this is all so very messed up." She placed a Sprite in Lance's hands. "Buy this for me, please. Ian, can we go outside and talk for just a minu—?"

"Whoa!" said Lance. "Look at *those*."

He nodded his head at a group of three undeniably cute girls.

They were laughing, swishing their hair in mesmerizing ways, and walking slowly toward the store. They almost seemed to be in soft focus, Ian thought, like models in shampoo commercials. *Except one of the girls is wearing a hat, which you probably wouldn't put in a shampoo ad.*

"Oh, come *on*, guys!" snapped Felicia. "Quit your panting, for God's sake. Creepball." Felicia whacked Lance on the shoulder lightly with the back of her hand.

"You know," he said, "that is not the first time you've hit me on this trip. You've got a violent streak. Anyway, I'm not ogling those girls for myself." He tapped Ian on the back. "Go get 'em, tiger."

"Huh?" Ian said.

"You need a confidence boost. And those chicks are it. Just go talk to them. I know you're feelin' all weird and smelly and orange and waxed. But don't let your confidence get all orange and, um . . . smelly." Ian and Felicia stared at him. "Okay, I lost my way a little there. Grammatically and metaphorically. The point is, you need to get back in the habit of projecting a certain arrogance, a casual hubris. An *attitude*. Now go talk to them."

Lance gave Ian another slight shove just as the girls entered the shop. They stared at him, whispering and giggling. Ian flashed back to the snickering little twits at Walgreens. *Lance is right*, he thought. *It is all about attitude. That's what's worked with Danielle. It can work anywhere.*

Lance shoved him again. Ian broke into a smooth stride and approached the girls. They were idly scanning a tall rack jammed with magazines.

"Hi!" he said in the artificially deep voice of fake Ian. The girls said nothing. They chewed gum with open mouths.

"So . . ." he said, taking another step toward them. "You girls like magazines?" He thought he heard Felicia gasp behind him but couldn't be sure.

"Yup," said the girl closest to Ian, popping a small bubble. "Are we in your way or something? Are you trying to get by?"

"No, no. Just checking out the, um . . . the reading material. Like you." He grabbed a map of South Carolina from a nearby display rack and began to examine it with feigned interest. He cleared his throat. "Are you girls from around here? You know, my friends and I are from Chicago, and we . . ."

When he turned around to gesture toward Felicia and Lance, he accidentally jabbed his thumb into the chest of a tall and inordinately muscular guy, flanked by two other equally menacing and inordinately muscular guys. The man stared at him coolly. He wore military dog tags, a backward baseball cap, and a sleeveless, unbuttoned flannel shirt.

"Excuse me," Ian said, no longer in his fake voice.

The man said nothing at first, then peered around Ian at the girls.

"Baby, who's your little orange friend here?"

One of the girls shrugged and shook her head, cracking her gum. "I dunno. Some guy," she said. "He was just saying how he likes reading material." The other girls laughed.

Boyfriends. Sure. Of course. This is how I die. It's all so clear.

The backward-hat man kept staring at Ian.

"What's that smell, guy? Is that *you*?"

"Oh, it's this stuff I have to wear. Medicine. For, um . . . for a skin condition. A rash. It's pretty contagious, actually. If it bothers you, I can easily move. Really. It's no trouble."

Ian stepped to his right, hoping to get back to his friends, back to his car, and back to the interstate. But one of the goons moved to block his path.

"You remind me of someone," said the backward-hat guy. "Oh yeah, I remember. The Great Pumpkin. From *Peanuts*. I love that one. 'It's the Great Pumpkin, Charlie Brown' or some shit."

The henchmen laughed. The girls half laughed. Ian didn't laugh at all. Then his Toady rang.

"Excuse me," he said. "Just one sec. I'd love to hear more. Really."

He checked the caller ID. It was Felicia.

"Hey, baby!" he said, returning to fake Ian mode.

"Wha–?" Felicia said in a whisper. "Oh, I get it. You still think those girls are going to buy your act. Sure. Okay. Well, can you get yourself out of that little mess you're in?"

"No, no," Ian said. "Just chillin'."

"You sound like a game show host when you use that voice, Ian. I don't like it. That voice has to stay behind when we leave South Carolina, okay?"

"Riiiiight," he said, rolling his eyes and smiling.

"God, you're a dork."

"Hey, where are you anyway, babe?"

"And don't call me 'babe,' either. I'm in the last aisle, crouched behind the hot dogs and nachos. Who get nachos at a gas station anyway? So gross."

"Oh, you're at Pedro's? Awesome! Yeah, I'd love to come over." Ian grinned an obnoxious, toothy grin. The girls' large boyfriends gathered around him as he spoke, blocking any obvious path of retreat.

"Are they moving, Ian? What's their deal? Are they going to let you out of here alive?"

"No, no." He kept smiling. "I doubt it. Sure, I can bring pizza."

"Excellent ruse. Really. You should be a secret agent or something. Listen, I have to go. Some bozo wants a hot dog. We're coming to get you."

Click.

Ian kept the phone pressed to his ear. "Okay," he said. "Can't wait to see you, babe. Buh-bye." He pressed end call and tucked the Toady back into his shorts.

"So," he said to the triumvirate of scary boyfriends. "I've gotta jet outta here. Got this thing tonight. A party. At Pedro's." He nodded at the backward-hat guy. "Good friend of mine, Pedro."

Felicia ducked between two of the giant boyfriends, snatched Ian's wrist, and led him quickly past the girls. She managed to bump each of the girls just enough to elicit small puffs of hostility from them. Felicia then raced down an aisle with Ian in tow, made a U-turn at a stack of Corona twelve-packs, and headed for the exit.

Again, Backward-hat's henchmen blocked the way.

"All right, what's the deal?" she asked them. "Are you keeping my friend a prisoner in the Sinclair? It's because he talked to your girlfriends over there, is that right? Is there some kind of boy chivalry thing going on here that I'm not privy to? What?" She edged close to one of the goons, still gripping Ian's arm. "Is there a password or something, Goober?" She poked him. "Talk to me, dummy."

He didn't. The backward-hat boy stared at Felicia.

"Who the hell are *you*?" he asked.

"And *what* are you?" She glared at him. "Look, sister, we were just gettin' to know your friend there. Seems like a nice guy. We don't meet too many orange people down here. . . ." His friends snickered "So we thought we'd introduce ourselves."

"Fine," said Felicia. "Introduce yourself, Ian."

"Hello," he said. His phone began to ring again. The large boyfriends seemed puzzled by this. So did Felicia.

"You get a lot of calls, man," said the backward-hat guy.

"He's very popular," said Felicia.

Ian assumed that this would be Lance calling. Somehow, he reasoned, Lance and Felicia planned to divert the goons' attention by incessantly calling his Toady. He couldn't quite divine the logic of that plan, but he thought he'd just roll with it. But it wasn't Lance calling at all.

Instead it was Becca, Ian's Dunkin' Donuts coworker.

"Hello?"

"Hey, Ian!" she chirped. "Surprised to hear from me I bet, huh?"

"Um . . . sure. I guess. What's going on, Becca?"

"Oh, nothin'."

"Well, great to hear from you Becca, but I'm kinda in the mid—"

"So listen, Ian. My date with Steve—the guy from the Gap—it was *awesome*. So awesome. Thanks for wearing that nasty old doughnut suit for me on Thursday. Ron is soooo pissed at you, by the way. But whatever. You're a peach. Thanks. Anyway, Steve wants me to go downtown with him and his friends tomorrow to, like, a baseball game or something. And I'm *dying* to go, Ian, but I'm totally on the schedule at work."

She paused. Ian stared at the large guys staring at him.

"That sucks, Becca. Sorry. Really. Listen, I'm really kind of occupied right now, so may—"

"Ian, could you maybe work for me tomorrow? I can totally cover for you sometime this week. Except Monday, 'cause I'm at the beach with Sara. Anyway, I'll switch some other day with you, Ian. Pleeeazzze…"

"Well, I would, Becca, but I'm out of town."

"You're *what?*"

"I'm nowhere near town, in fact." Felicia looked at Ian with the same puzzled expression that had taken over the faces of the squad of giant boyfriends. "So I really can't cover for you, Becca. Sorry. Maybe you could call in sick or something."

"Oh please, Ian. I'll do any—"

"Later, Becca."

Click.

"Sorry," said Ian. "Again. That's so rude, I know." The goons eyed him suspiciously. "It was this girl from work. Schedule conflict. It's like you can leave the office, but, um . . . the office always, um . . . manages to track you down." He cleared his throat. "Heh-heh. My dad always says that. He's a dentist, my dad."

Just then, the gum-chewing magazine girls began to laugh. They weren't laughing at Ian, either. They were gathered around Lance near a cooler full of RC Cola at the store's entrance. He was apparently saying something witty and charming. Two of them were giggling and blushing. The third girl placed her hand on Lance's forearm and leaned in close, smiling bright and wide. She withdrew a pen from a small, sequined clutch purse, then jotted something down on a gum wrapper and slipped it inside Lance's hand.

This flirtatious exchange drew the attention of nearly everyone in the Sinclair. It drew the unmistakable ire of the backward-cap boyfriend, too. He and his goons began walking toward the girls, eyeing the new apparent threat. Lance, smiling as he stuffed the gum wrapper into a pocket, picked his head up, looked at Felicia and Ian, and mouthed the word *go*.

"Please excuse me for a moment, ladies," he said to the gum-chewers, then spun on his heels and sprinted toward the Creature.

Felicia and Ian tore out of the store behind him. Lance hopped into the passenger seat, Felicia dove behind the wheel, and Ian—after screwing on the Creature's gas cap and resetting the pump—flew into the back. Felicia peeled out of the Sinclair noisily. Two of the goons stood just outside the store's entrance glaring furiously, but the backward-hat guy—their apparent leader—lagged behind to interrogate his girlfriend.

"Just another routine escape," said Lance, still huffing from the run to the car. "Ho-hum. Yawn. Nothing unusual about it anymore, really. It just seems to be the way we choose to leave most settings."

"*That* was a freakin' nightmare," said Ian.

"Oh, stop being such a *wuss*, Ian," chided Felicia. "Has it occurred to you that maybe *you*, Ian Lafferty, bring some of these things on? Lance totally saved your ass back there." She extended a hand toward the passenger seat and gave Lance a low five. "I've got to admit, Nesbitt, that was an excellent use of your flirting skills. Very resourceful. It's not often—if ever—that I find that talent helpful."

"Thank you very much, thank you . . ." said Lance.

"Oh, you are *kidding* me!" said Ian. "That whole near-violent disaster happened because of Lance's preoccupation with every girl that he can possibly detect on his babe radar. We got in that mess *because* of him."

"We did?" asked Felicia and Lance in unison. They low-fived again.

"Dude," said Lance. "I think you need to back off that statement. We got in that mess because you were a wreck around those girls—"

"And then you were an über-wuss with those meathead guys," added Felicia. "*That* is why I ended up crouched behind a batch of hot dogs trying to figure out a way to rescue you, and *that* is why we found ourselves in that near-violent disaster." She paused. "You really showed some stones with that Becca person, though."

Ian muttered and grumbled in the backseat as the Creature hurtled southeast down I-26.

"'You need a confidence boost,' Lance says. 'Just go talk to them,' Lance says. So of course I do. Stupid, stupid, stupid."

"Oh, c'mon. I thought it would be nice for you to practice the whole bizarre-Ian thing with a few girls who were totally unknown and thus who should have seemed unintimidating. Because in just an hour or so, you—still in the guise of bizarre Ian—will be trying to have *sex* with a girl you've never met. And that might be slightly more intimidating."

Ian sulked.

"You know something, Ian?" said Felicia. "It might just be possible that you're no good at being anything other than Ian Lafferty, incredibly nice guy. That's why you're tripping all over yourself with these truck-stop hussies and their weaselly boyfriends. You're not any good at being a fraud, Ian. You're having trouble pulling off the tan and the haircut and the weirdo deep voice and the slick talk because that's *not you*. Clearly you'd like to be good at it. Clearly you feel some sort of gender-related instinctual urge to get it on with hot girls. Whatever, dork. But in the end, you're this nice, sweet person who just can't hustle bimbos." She paused. "And I like that."

Still Ian sulked.

"Hey, gimme that Sprite," Felicia said. Lance popped open the can, and she sipped it cautiously. "So what'd that girl give you back there?" she asked Lance. "The world's shortest suicide note?"

"Just her phone number and her IM name. No big thing."

"And you kept it?"

"Sure."

"Why?"

"Because you never know."

"You never know what?"

"You just never know. If I had thought to ask for Elise's phone number five years ago back at the Birdeye Creek Science Camp, who knows what might've happened?"

"It's still tough to imagine you having a steady girl, Lance."

"She was the one. Anyway, I get the numbers because you just never know."

Ian unscrewed the Old Spice and splashed several drops onto his hands, then applied it to his neck and face. He cringed as it began to sting.

"Ugh," groaned Lance.

"Wearing that crap isn't much better than smelling like old dog. Now you smell like . . . mmmm . . ." He sniffed the air that wafted from the backseat. "You smell like lighter fluid and sweaty socks, Ian. Not good. I can't really say this is helping. I've read a lot about women and pheromones and smells and stuff. They like a pleasant-smelling guy, not an *abusively* smelling guy."

Felicia laughed, then said, "I don't know. This is probably right for fake Ian. Yeah, I think fake Ian is *exactly* the sort of stud who would douse himself in sewer water if it had a little sailboat on the bottle."

"Fake Ian says nuts to you." The real Ian kept up his sulking.

He slid the sunglasses onto his face and rested his head. He was exhausted. Very little sleep and excessive fretting had him wound far too tight. Curiously, Felicia and Lance seemed completely at ease. They cracked jokes about the Sinclair goons and debated their Charleston itinerary. Felicia wanted to see historic homes, then sleep; Lance wanted to reach the nightlife as quickly as possible, then party. They passed more mileage signs for the city. Whatever they were going to do, it wouldn't be long before they were doing it. And Ian's moment of truth with Danielle was fast approaching. Or rather, another moment of *un*truth with Danielle was fast approaching. Whatever. Anyway, it meant the near-certainty of sex if Ian didn't botch things up. Or if nothing else went wrong in the remaining forty miles or so.

He sent Danielle another text message:

w8 up 4 me

She soon responded:

gr8 party! Plz hurry! im w8ing. . . .

Somehow, this only made Ian more uptight. A sense of dread had crept over him. He felt certain that Danielle would be gone when he arrived. Or she'd be drunk beyond comprehension. Or she'd simply be disappointed in him. He slunk further into the cushy rear seat of the Creature.

"Hey, um, Ian," said Felicia. "Have all these little red dashboard lights been on the whole trip, or is this something new?"

Ian shot forward. The Creature's oil and engine indicator lights were both illuminated.

"No," he said. "That's definitely new."

"So should I pull off the road?" Felicia asked.

Something underneath the hood began to rattle. Loudly. Then a faint whistling developed. It soon became a high-pitched wail. Felicia began to slow the car down.

"We can't just stop along the interstate," Ian said.

"Why?" she asked. "We'll call Triple A or something. Get a tow truck."

"Look, we can't stop *now*," Ian said, raising his voice.

"Well, maybe we should call my parents and—"

"Hey!" snapped Ian. With his new high-arched eyebrows, he looked absolutely petrified, and maybe a little unhinged. "We are definitely *not* calling parents. We are a looooonng way from calling parents, okay? Just remain calm!"

"You mean like you?" asked Felicia.

"No, I mean like . . . well, like someone much calmer than me. Just be calm, that's all. And whatever you do, keep driving."

So she did. The Creature continued along near the speed limit for approximately ten miles in the black of night. They were, Ian thought, the longest ten miles of his life. Until the next ten miles arrived. Then the car wouldn't crack forty miles per hour as it maneu-vered through a thickening nighttime mist. Other motorists flew past. The Creature's heat gauge was maxed out, its needle well past the *H* and buried in a zone of red that indicated only bad things.

"Your engine is going to explode," said Lance. "The Creature's overheated. Like, waaaay overheated."

"You should actually turn the heater on, Felicia," said Ian. "All the way. It's one of my dad's classic car trip strategies. Supposedly it draws heat away from the engine, so we don't, like, break down. Or blow up."

"This is insane," she said. "I'm totally getting off at the next exit."

"Dude, I think the next exit is practically in Charleston," said Lance.

The were, in fact, very close. They were already seeing signs for the Charleston airport. The next exit would be within proverbial spittin' distance of Danielle, Ian thought.

White smoke began to seep from the hood of the Creature. Feli-cia flipped off the air conditioner and put the heat on full blast as Ian had instructed. This seemed to lessen the intolerable whistling noise but did nothing to quiet the Creature's ferocious rattling.

"A death rattle," Felicia called it.

To say that Ian's car *limped* into downtown Charleston would be a gross insult to the pace of most limpers. It crawled and gasped heroically at no more than twenty miles an hour in the final hour of its useful life, smoke pouring from its ancient hood. Other drivers should have applauded the dying car's grit and determination.

Instead, they honked, screamed expletives, and repeatedly gave Felicia the finger.

She was in no mood to receive the finger, either. With the heat on high, the Creature was a crucible. Ian, Lance, and Felicia were soaked in sweat. Rolling the car windows down offered little relief, since breathing the South Carolina air was like sucking down hot broth. But the Creature chugged on, toward the bright lights of the city.

Its final parking place was an illegal one, at the corner of Queen and Meeting streets, near the southern tip of the peninsula that contained the city. Felicia threw the Creature into park and listened to it sputter for another minute. Then something popped loudly under the hood. The Creature emitted a hiss of white smoke, like a last breath, then went silent. She clicked the key in the ignition to no avail. It was just after 11 P.M.

"Damn," said Lance, exiting the car. "At least we're here. I can't believe we actually made it." He pulled his sweat-soaked shirt away from his chest and shook it briskly.

Ian eased himself out of the car and slammed the door, then reached in the driver's side window and pulled a latch below the dashboard that opened the Creature's trunk. "Please remove all of your belongings." He snatched his backpack and the plastic bag with the vomit-stained doughnut costume.

"Huh?" said Felicia.

"We leave the car and start walking."

"What do you mean 'leave the car'?" asked Lance, clearly shocked.

"As in, we're going on and it's not. As in, we abandon it by the side of the road. As in, *hasta la vista*, Creature." Ian slung his backpack over his shoulder, then tossed Lance and Felicia their belongings.

"But, Ian," said Felicia. "It's your *car*."

"It only cost three hundred and fifty dollars. Like Lance tells me all the time, it's practically disposable. So I'm disposing of it. And anyway, if I never see the inside of that thing again, I'll be okay. You know what it reminds me of? Three things: work, school, and being completely exhausted *after* work or school."

"I think that's four things, dude."

"Whatever. I don't like any of them. It reminds me of this doomed trip, too. That is *not* a point in the car's favor." He wrapped the doughnut costume in a second plastic bag, then tucked it in an unused pocket of his backpack. "Let's go, guys."

"Um . . . how are we going to go anywhere without the car?"

"We walk. We're not far from Danielle's campus, really. It's maybe like a mile or so." He paused. Felicia seemed distressed. "We're surrounded by historic shit here, Felicia. It could be a *nice* walk."

"How will we get home?" she asked.

"Amtrak. There's a train every day. Or maybe Greyhound. There's always a bus. I've got plenty of Dunkin' Donuts profits in the bank to cover our fares. Don't worry, Felicia."

"Isn't your dad going to freak about the car?" asked Lance.

"Yes. There's no question. I think we need to tell him I sold it."

"*Sold* it?" asked Felicia. "Who would buy it?"

"Lance's cousin Doug."

"Doug? He never has *beer* money, let alone the cash for a ca—"

"Not the point. We just tell my dad that Doug offered me, like, four hundred dollars and I took it. If he thinks I made fifty bucks on a beater of a car that's older than me, he'll hug me and never question the transaction."

"Won't the city of Charleston eventually tow this thing, then start sending a bunch of notices to your house?" asked Felicia.

"That's really Doug's problem," answered Ian.

Felicia and Lance stared at each other, a bit bewildered.

"Can we *please* go now?" Ian said.

They began to walk, passing Charleston's rows of stately old houses, many adorned with intricate railings, elaborate columns, latticework and leaded-glass windows. It felt otherworldly to the three suburbanites. Well, it felt otherworldly to two of them, and if Ian had been paying any attention to his surroundings, it would have felt otherworldly to him, too. But he was busy attempting to text Danielle. She, however, wasn't responding.

That's it. I've soooo blown it. By the time I get to her front door, it'll be midnight, she'll be passed out somewhere, and I'll have to—no, Lance, Felicia and I will all *have to find someplace to stay. God knows where. And I will almost certainly not be having sex. And why does Felicia have to keep calling me* "wuss" *and* "über-wuss"*? I don't like that.*

"Are we almost there?" asked Lance.

"It's not far. Try to keep up the pace."

A rather large insect buzzed past Felicia. She yelped, swatted at the air with her hands, then lurched forward and fell into a gardenia, spilling her beverage. "Did you guys *see* that frickin' thing?!" she exclaimed. "Jeee-*zuhs!*"

"Palmetto bug," said Ian flatly, helping her to her feet.

"It looked like a flying rat!"

"It's not much different. It's a winged cockroach. Might be the state bird down here."

Felicia nearly heaved again. They kept walking until they reached the South Carolina Southern University campus. Then Ian quickened his pace. Lance's head was set on "swivel." "Dude, the women are amazing down here! And the thing is, they've all gotta be relatively smart to be here, don't they? Holy crapballs!"

When they began to encounter houses displaying Greek letters, Ian broke into a jog. "We're looking for George Street," he called out. "It's the Sigma Tau Delta house."

"Good thing we've all had some advanced math," said Felicia, not quite keeping up with him. "My Greek isn't really the best." She stopped, unable to run in her sick state and in the crushing heat. "I'm sweating through my shoes!" she yelled. "Once again I feel the need to remind you: sick girl on board."

Fortunately for her, Ian had stopped, too. He stood on the wide sidewalk in front of a beautiful old double-gallery home with the letters ΣΤΔ above the doorway. A long banner was suspended between two upstairs windows:

¡BUENA SUERTE, DANIELLE! GOOD LUCK! ? YOUR SISTERS

"Guess this is the place, eh?" asked Lance.

Ian nodded. "Guess so."

Partygoers were strewn across the front lawn of the sorority house, some dancing, most drinking, and a few apparently passed out.

"Dude," said a grinning Lance. "These are the most attractive people I have seen in my entire life. Oh my."

"You can't stay," said Ian. "Find your own hot sorority. This one's mine."

"Dude! You've already got a girl in there. C'mon, you can't just expect me to *leave*."

"Oh, that's exactly what I expect," said Ian, turning to face Lance.

"Boys, boys . . ." said Felicia, lumbering up slowly beside them. "I'm sure you can find a way to share the girls. There's one for Ian, and . . . let's see . . . one, two, three . . . about forty of them for Lance. That should keep him entertained until morning. I'll just find a nice bed or a couch in there to sleep on. With all this revelry going on, nobody will notice. I probably won't even have to join their house."

"You guys are *not* coming in," declared Ian firmly. His orange face was wet with perspiration. He did, in fact, smell like some combination of dog, sock, and lighter fluid. His high-arching eyebrows lent his face a wild-eyed insanity that was normally absent.

"What's your deal?" Lance placed a hand on Ian's shoulder, but Ian pulled away.

"My *deal* is that I should be here *alone*. I knew bringing you two was a mistake. When you're not delaying me, you're insulting me." He took a few steps that led to the sorority's front door. Two sloshed coeds with plastic cups in their hands walked between Ian and Lance, smiling. It was all Lance could do to remain in the conversation.

"Um . . . dude. I thought we were having fun. I mean, even with all the headaches and puking and bad haircuts and angry boyfriends and brushes with the law—well, I've had fun."

"I kinda have, too," said Felicia. "But I could have done without the puking."

"This was just supposed to be, like, a Lance-a-Palooza road trip. Like how they always have *The Real World* in a different city. I was thinking maybe we could take Lance-a-Palooza to, say, Miami next year. Or New Orleans. Or New York. Or Bos—"

"This is not a thing like *The Real World*, Lance! This is fake Ian's world! This trip was about me getting myself out of the house, out of the mall! This trip was about me doing something remotely adventurous just once in my freakin' life! This trip was also about me finally getting somewhere with a girl—an actual live girl! No, not someone who I necessarily *love*, per se—not that I couldn't—or even someone who knows the real me. Whoever that is. Anyway, she wouldn't even *like* the real me. No girl seems to. To most girls I know, the *real* Ian Lafferty is only useful for covering a shift at work, or borrowing notes from in a class, or taking care of whatever lame-ass thing she doesn't want to deal with. I'm just an f'ing tool, Lance." Ian paused. "But with Danielle, it's different."

"Yeah, it's a big lie," said Felicia. "So that's different."

"But like Lance has said, you've gotta admit it *worked*."

"I thought this end-of-summer trip was about three friends—three very good friends who've gotten through everything together since, like, kindergarten—trying to reconnect and have some fun. I've totally missed you guys." Lance had a genuinely insulted expression. "Isn't that maybe a little more important than whether you get some from this chick you've totally been *playing*?"

"Obviously Ian doesn't think so," said Felicia grimly.

"Look, I told you guys from the start that I thought I should do this alone."

"Actually, you told us from the start that your grandma was sick, dude."

They were silent for a moment.

"Look, I want you guys to have a good time in Charleston," said Ian. "But you can't do it here, not at Danielle's house." He reached into his wallet, pulled out a wad of twenties, and pressed them into Lance's hand. "It's all the cash I have on me. Use it for bus or plane or train fare—whatever. I'm sorry I can't drive you guys back. I'll take Amtrak home tomorrow. And I guess I'll have to call my manager—

who'll probably fire me, but I don't really care. My dad might care, but I can appease him." Ian sighed. "I've gotta go."

He took a step toward the sorority.

"Wait, Ian," said Felicia. "There's something else. I just wanna tell you something. I've—"

"What else?!" he said, spinning around. "What haven't I heard? Let's run through the list: 'You're doing this for all the wrong reasons, Ian.' And 'Your hair is all wrong, Ian.' And 'Your eyebrows are too bushy, Ian.' And 'You're making a mistake that you're bound to regret, Ian.' And 'Try to think of something yucky while you have sex, Ian. Like your dad.' I think that was my favorite. Oh, there's also 'Stop being a wuss, Ian.' That was a good one. And of course there's 'I have to pee, Ian.' And 'Wanna cheesy popover, Ian?'" He looked at Felicia almost bitterly. "So what exactly do you wanna tell me *now*?!"

She was clearly shaken.

"I, um . . . " She tried to remain composed. "I just wanted to remind you to wear your mango condom, big guy."

She turned and walked toward the street. Ian headed for the sorority's front door.

Various women of Sigma Tau Delta eyed Ian curiously as he walked up the path that led to their front door. He thought he heard the words *orange*, *stanky*, and *tweezed* being whispered, but he couldn't be certain. He looked only at the doorway, trying not to think about the two friends whose company he'd just left. A tall, thin blonde met him on the sorority's front porch, just as he was about to walk through the open door.

"Can I help you? I'm afraid this is a bit of a private party, actually, and—"

"I'm a friend of Danielle's," he said. "I've driven a long way to be here, too. And my car is dead, and my friends are pissed at me, and, well . . . do you know where I can find Danielle?"

"You're not Ian, are you?"

"Yup, 'fraid so."

"Well, shoot," said the sorority girl. "She's cried her eyes out about you a few times. I don't know whether I should slap you or hug you." She stepped closer toward Ian, clearly noticing his sweatiness and his scent. "I believe I'll just shake your hand. Hi, Ian. I'm Madison."

She led Ian inside the house. The interior was stunning: an elegant chandelier hung over the foyer, oil paintings in gold-leaf frames lined the walls, and the vintage furnishings all seemed far too pretty to actually use. Madison took him into the sorority's kitchen, where he sat in a stiff-backed chair at a small table.

"I'll run upstairs and get Danielle. She's got a pretty early flight, so she might be in bed already. But more likely she's just crying to one of her girlfriends about you. Anyway, wait right here."

He did.

I was much too harsh with Felicia. That was unnecessary. No, it was selfish. That whole display was selfish. Man, I can be a jerk. And it's all just so I can hook up with some strange girl. Good grief. How could I— Oh shit, Ian. Snap out of this. Danielle will be downstairs any second, and then fake Ian has to dazzle. He tapped his feet nervously. *Yeesh, I was hard on Felicia. The poor thing's been sick and—*

"Ian?"

Danielle stood in the kitchen's small doorway, wearing small white boxers and a pink satin spaghetti-strap top that subtly exposed her perfectly flat abdomen. *Whoa,* thought Ian. *The beach pictures did not do her justice.* Danielle was the most attractive person he'd ever been anywhere near. In fact, she was more attractive than any person he'd ever even fantasized about. Her skin was bronze and flawless. Her eyes were warm and gleaming. *Oh my.*

Danielle raced toward him. She jumped on his lap and threw her arms around his neck. He ran his hands over her smooth bare shoulders and realized immediately that there was nothing he could possibly think of—not his dad, not Ron, not the scary hayseed goons at the Sinclair—that would prevent his . . . well, his Twizzler from becoming, say, a Super Rope.

"I'm soooo happy to see you," she said. She snuggled against him and ran her hand inside his T-shirt. She kissed him. He kissed her back. Incredibly, she seemed undeterred by his recently altered appearance. Not even his strange orange hue or his inhuman eyebrows distracted her.

I really should have been more considerate of Lance's and Felicia's feelings. What an ass I am. They've shown me more loyalty than I deser— Oh hell, Ian. Kiss the girl. Don't screw this up.

After several seconds of impassioned smooching, Danielle's lips broke away.

"What took you so long, Ian? I thought I'd see you yesterday! I was so worried you met some other girl on the road, you flirt."

"Well, Tasty," he said, trying to project fake Ian's confidence and asshole-ishness, "I did have a few diversions. But I wasn't going to blow you off."

They kissed again.

I bet it's ninety-five degrees outside, easy. And Felicia's been so dehydrated. And she spilled her Sprite all over that gardenia. Hope she gets some water somewhere. She really should— Aargh. Dammit, Ian, keep kissing the impossibly hot babe on your lap. *Do not* screw this up.

Periodically, Danielle would pause to make small talk, usually in an effort to tease a compliment out of her ostensibly cool and inconsiderate cyber-boyfriend. Fake Ian played it perfectly, saying just enough to earn more kissing, but not enough to let Danielle believe she had him hooked. "So what is it you want to see while you're in Charleston, baby?" she asked. "We've still got a few hours together."

"Why don't you show me your room," answered fake Ian.

She smiled coquettishly. "We're not supposed to have boys upstairs. It's a rule."

"What can they do, kick you out?" asked fake Ian. "You leave tomorrow. And anyway, babe, I'm not a little *boy*."

Oh God. That was a stupid thing to say. That was soap-opera and sitcom stupid. No, that was porn stupid. Felicia would be rolling. There's just no way that Danielle will buy that half-assed line. . . .

But she did, it seemed. Danielle took his orange hand and led him up a back stairwell, tiptoeing silently and peeking around corners so as to avoid detection by the sisterhood. She shoved him into her room, then onto her bed. She brushed a collection of stuffed bears off her comforter, then wrapped her legs around Ian's waist and shut off her bedside light.

"Well, this is my room," she said. "Anything else you'd like to see?"

Okay, Felicia wouldn't think this part was so funny.

They began to kiss again. Every time they did, Ian thought of the Pabst/plastic deer disaster. He didn't want to think about it, but he did. *Of all nights, why would I get shitfaced drunk then? How could I blow that? Man, that was dumb. If only I hadn't— Ack. Stop. Kiss the girl on the bed, Ian. Kiss the girl. . . .*

Ian's hands slid inside Danielle's pink satin top. It felt unreal. Almost dreamlike. She was perfect. Soon, Ian was touching a bra. *A bra. Good God, a real live bra.* By the feel of things, it was a lacy bra, too. Something sexy for its own sake, even when it didn't contain boobs. Of course, the bra that Ian was touching *did* contain boobs. Danielle said, "Oh, Ian," in a slow whisper. He felt his heart race.

Why, then, could he not stop thinking about his friends?

That was just wrong, walking away like that. Dumb and wrong. Felicia's sick. Has she ever been anything but a perfect friend? No.

Danielle lifted off the pink top, then removed Ian's shirt. Part of him was unimaginably turned on. But at the same time, another part of him—some emotional center—was sounding an internal alarm, telling Ian that he was in the wrong place and with the wrong girl. By the standards of the average seventeen-year-old male, of course, Danielle was the ideal female: perfectly curved, sweet-voiced, and deferential. And in the darkness atop her bed, she seemed to have a very good idea of what to do. But, Ian realized, he didn't necessarily want whatever the average seventeen-year-old guy was supposed to want. Something about the encounter with Danielle just felt wrong, badly syncopated, ill-conceived. *Something just doesn't . . . fit,* Ian thought.

He recalled Felicia's words at the clinic: "We fit very well together, Ian."

Yes, they did.

Ian snatched a shirt from the bed and untangled himself from Danielle.

"Sorry, hon," he said. "There's something I really need to do. *Now.*"

"Wha—? Ian, what's wrong?" she said. "You didn't— Oh, I know. This happens to lots of guys, Ian. It's okay. Please stay!"

He was gone. Ian thundered down the stairs and began to put on the shirt—but he'd inadvertently grabbed Danielle's pink satin top. "Oh, screw it," he said, running past blond-haired Madison. "I've lost a car today, I can lose a lousy shirt." He tossed the pink top onto the ΣΤΔ lawn and raced down the front steps of the porch.

Danielle's head appeared in an upstairs window.

"Ian!" she called. "What's wrong?" He didn't answer. Too much was wrong, and he needed to make it right. Danielle yelled again, "Oh, you smelled weird anyway!"

Ian didn't have to run very far to find Lance. In fact, he took no more than six or seven steps. Lance was flirting with a pair of very drunk, wobbly girls on the sidewalk just in front of the sorority house.

"So, yeah," he was saying. "That's when I changed my major to biomedical engineering. I figure that if my research can just save one life—just *one*—maybe then the nightmares will—"

"Lance!" yelled Ian. "Thank God I found you!"

"Oh, hey, Ian. You finished already? That was quick, mango man. Tough luck. But hey, I'd like you to meet Missy and Kristen. Girls, this is the friend I was telling you about. He's prelaw. Even though he's shirtless right now, I'm telling you, Ian is one of the smartest—"

"Lance, I *have* to know where Felicia is!" Ian was panicked. "She's not gone, is she? Tell me she didn't just run off!"

"Dude, chill. She's in no condition to run anyway. Excuse me, ladies." Lance wrapped an arm around Ian's bare shoulders and led him away from the intoxicated coeds. "Just because things may not

have gone perfectly for you in there—what with the girl hanging out
the window screaming at you and all—well, that doesn't mean you
have to F things up for me with these hotties. What's your deal?"

"Sorry, Lance. And I'm really sorry for being such an ass earlier.
But right now, I have *got* to find Felicia. There's something—no, there
are *several* things that I need to tell her."

"Oh, you mean about how you love her and you've always loved
her and you can't believe it took you so long to admit it?"

"Yeah, I've got to— I'm sorry, *what?*" Ian took a step back. "I mean,
how do you know all that?"

"People skills. What, you think I get chicks just because I'm a
good-looking guy?"

"No," said Ian. "No, I was always pretty confident that couldn't
be it."

Lance laughed.

"Felicia started walking back to the car right after you yelled at her
like a total maniac," he said. "I don't think she wanted these sorority
girls to see her cry."

"Why didn't you go with her?"

"Well, she made it pretty clear that she didn't want me to see her
cry, either. She said she needed to walk, needed to clear her head."

"Why on earth would she go to the car? It's dead."

"I dunno. Maybe because it reminds her of Ian Lafferty before he
got all sex-crazy." He turned around to make sure the coeds were still
nearby. "Look, I'm sure you can find her. She wasn't moving too fast.
Now, if you don't mind, I have to finish telling these girls about my
internship at a leading biotechnology company."

"You amaze me. You frighten me, too."

"It's a gift. Now run."

That's precisely what Ian did. He bolted past the sorority houses, a look of crazed desperation on his recently waxed face. He wove through groups of frat boys returning from bars and leaped over curbside flowerbeds. His second trip through Charleston's historic old neighborhoods was much like his first. That is to say, he saw none of the intrinsic beauty of the city's architecture or its flora. His mind was on a girl. But this time, he felt certain that his mind was on the *right* girl. He passed the shrub into which Felicia had fallen. He smiled at first, but then his pulse accelerated and he grew worried.

What if something else happens to her? After all, she's not well. What if she faints? It's seriously hot down here. God, I'd never forgive myself. Ian dialed Felicia's cell phone. She didn't answer.

The Creature soon came into view. It already had a parking ticket under its passenger-side wiper blade—one that Ian had no intention of taking home with him—and a red municipal parking boot on a rear tire. At first glance, Ian thought that Felicia wasn't there. He saw nothing but the great hulking mass of yellow-painted steel that was his useless car.

But then he heard a girl's sigh and noticed a silhouette atop the Creature. Felicia was reclining on the trunk, resting her head against the angled glass of the rear windshield. Ian broke into a sprint.

"Felicia!" he called.

She didn't move. He called out again, then skidded to a halt by the rear fender. Felicia looked at him blankly. In her hands, she held the crappily constructed tongue-depressor-and-latex-glove dog that Ian had crafted at the clinic.

Ian was breathless.

"You have no shirt," Felicia said. "Did the girl take it? Maybe she keeps trophies from all of her Internet victims. How was it? Was she everything you'd hoped she'd–?"

"Oh, shut up," Ian said. "We didn't do it. I mean, we started to do it, but . . ." He stalled. There was just so much to say. "So what did you *really* want to tell me? Outside the sorority house. When I was being a total jackass. Were you actually concerned that I wouldn't use any protection? Because of course I intended to. I'm no fool."

"Yes, you are. And no, that is not what I was going to say. But I don't feel very much like saying what I had intended to say right at this moment." She rolled her head to the side, facing away from Ian. He scrambled over the Creature's rear bumper so that he could look her in the eye.

"Whatever it was, I have some things to say to you. And I'm not going to wuss out. And I haven't had a thing to drink, so there will be no incidents with any lawn ornaments, not tonight." Felicia closed her eyes and smiled. "The thing is, I don't actually know *why* I pursued this stupid, stupid Danielle business. Maybe it was the sense of control. Maybe it was impulsiveness of it all–that's not normally one of my trademarks. Maybe it was that she is *really* freakin' hot. I mean, you should see this girl. Unbelie–"

She frowned at him.

"I think you're maybe going off on an ill-advised tangent there, Ian."

"Right." He paused. "Well, anyway, it wasn't some pure sex thing. I think I just felt lost all summer. Away from you guys." He looked at the ground, then back at Felicia. Her dark eyes reflected the white moon. "Especially away from you."

They exchanged a nervous look.

"This has been a goofy trip," Ian continued. "Cops, llamas, angry hick boyfriends. Even though I'm left smelling like an old farty dog, and, well, you've been disgustingly sick, this has been a *great* trip. I've figured some things out. Things I probably should have known for years. I'm maybe in love here, Felicia. Or at least I'm in a desperate state of serious liking. And not with that Internet ho, either." He inched closer. "I think maybe with you."

She smiled at him, ditching the tongue-depressor dog.

"So now what do we do about it?" he asked.

She pulled him onto the trunk. They kissed.

"We get you a new goddamn haircut, that's the first thing we do," she said after several seconds. "And perhaps a more natural tan."

A palmetto bug alighted on the car. Felicia squawked in terror and they rolled to the curb with a thud. They kissed again in the grass.

"Oh, Ian," she whispered.

This fits.

This day is going unusually well, thought Ian.

He was reclining on the soft gray fabric of his seat on the 1:45 Amtrak train to Washington, D.C., where, after a two-hour layover, he would catch another train to Chicago. Felicia had curled herself into a snug ball, resting her head on his lap. He stroked her hair. Lance slept in a seat across the aisle. Ian dialed a number on his Toady.

"Dunkin' Donuts, this is Ron. How can I help you?"

"Hey, Ron."

"Ian? Is that you? Listen, Becca was very upset this morning. She tells me that she asked you to sub for her and you refused. Now Ian, we need team players here. That's how you get ahead in the business world, Ian. Think of what's best fo–"

"Listen, Ron, I wish I could talk longer, but I just can't. I called to tell you that I'm quitting."

Ron fell silent for a moment.

"Y-y-you're what?" he finally stammered. "You can't just quit, Ian. You're on the schedule tomorrow. I need you here by six thirty! What about giving me two weeks noti–?"

"Ron, buddy, I wish I could. I really do. But I'm not going to be home until tomorrow. Late. This was really some kind of crazy weekend. Anyway, school is starting and, well . . . I just have different priorities now, Ron. Sorry to disappoint you."

Ron was silent for several more seconds. Ian thought he heard his former manager chewing but couldn't be certain.

"Actually, a series of things has happened. Let's just say you should probably deduct the cost of the suit from my last check. And you might want to call the regional manager about getting a new doughnut, too."